# The Writings of Owen Wister

of The American Academy of Arts and Letters

Membre Correspondant de la Société
des Gens de Lettres

Honorary Fellow of the Royal Society of Literature

===

# U. S. Grant

## and

# The Seven Ages of Washington

# PREFACE—*Success and the Cash-Box*

IN *Babel* for the year 1901 is stored a harvest of printed and private comment concerning the short biography of General Grant, which might lead an innocent person to conclude that wealth beyond the dreams of avarice had rolled in upon its fortunate author. It cost the author about eight months of hard labor, it was published late in 1900, and, had he limited himself to three a day, its proceeds, carefully hoarded, might possibly have kept him in cigarettes these twenty-eight years. Providentially, the author does not smoke cigarettes, and hence was not deterred from spending some eight or nine months more in 1907 upon a short biography of Washington. This second venture outside the field of fiction did drop a few more pennies in the cash-box; but when William Roscoe Thayer urged that fiction be abandoned henceforth for biography, it couldn't be thought of: eight times since Grant appeared, requests to write biographies have had to be declined.

Mr. James Ford Rhodes pays this small work the compliment of referring to it in his great work. Mr. Joseph Choate thought that my mention of Grant's infirmity was a mistake. I can't find among the letters and newspaper cuttings preserved in

*Babel*, that anyone else was of this opinion. Mr. Charles Francis Adams referred me to a sketch of Grant in the winter of 1863–64, by Richard H. Dana, which, had I seen it during the eight months of hard labor, would have helped me to make Grant more vivid in that momentous hour of his destiny. At the end of the second letter which he wrote me about Grant, Senator Lodge says in reply to one from me, in which I had given him my authority for a statement about paper money:

". . . I know of course, that no book like that could be written without study behind every sentence. When one is condensing, as you were obliged to do there, you have to read a number of books in order to write a single paragraph. You understand, of course, that I do not defend irredeemable currency, but I am quite sure that there are cases where it is necessary, and that our War of the Rebellion was one of these necessities, just as the Napoleonic wars were to England. The painful business of getting back to specie payments is simply part of the price that a nation has to pay for carrying through a desperate struggle. Horace White would not take that view, but he is not the kind of man who saves nations by opening dykes or other desperate cures for desperate times. He only criticizes those who do—a common type. . . ."

It's evident from *Babel* that more than one of

my statements in Grant brought discussion from
Cabot Lodge and Roosevelt, and that I seem to have
given them my authorities by way of justification.

Here is one of Roosevelt's letters:

". . . I do not know precisely what point
Lodge made about Condé and Charles XI in connection with Sheridan, but from curiosity I have
been looking up their careers and I want to say,
in the first place, that I appreciate better than I
did why you selected them for comparison with
Sheridan; and in the next place, that I feel they
will loom larger in the history of the military art.
I think the comparison to be made or implied in
connection with them is but very partial, but each
belonged to the dashing order of generals—to the
type that strikes quick and hard and always strives
to get the drop on the adversary. I think that
Sheridan at the end was a greater general than
either Condé or the Swede was at the end, for
Sheridan grew, while an astounding thing about
each of the others is that he was at his best at the
beginning and fell off afterwards. But I do not
think that Sheridan's best was ever equal to the
best of either the Swede or the Frenchman. . . ."

I find on a review of the newspaper cuttings—
some of them honored the small book with a column
—that the opening paragraph of Grant is quoted
entire several times. It concludes with the sentence:

"All the neighbors know his face to-day," which, in the Italian translation, published some years later in Florence, becomes

"Oggi l'imagine sua è scolpita nel cuore di tutti,"

and this, brought back to English, is

"To-day his likeness is carved upon the heart of all."

That is, in its general sense, a faithful equivalent of the original—yet, is it not a pretty example of how in the process of transmuting a piece of one language into a piece of another, something elusive escapes, evaporates, is lost?—especially between northern and latin idioms?

About the biography of Washington nothing need be quoted from *Babel*, except that when Henry Adams wrote asking for more of this, for expansion in the same vein, suggesting further distillation from Washington's letters and diaries, the cash-box gave forth a hollow negative. The best part of a year's study and labor, and fewer pennies for it than for one short story written in less than a month? Bad business!

Looking back, did it pay, this exacting devotion, lavished on two portraits of great Americans? Were those eighteen months of Grant and Washington spent, or squandered?

The most illustrious best seller that ever lived

answered this question over a hundred years ago, when he used to declare that "literature should be a staff and not a crutch."

To a courteous correspondent during the past year, I owe a correction. In a quotation from one of Washington's youthful letters, the word *Matchcoat* occurs. "Should not this be *Watchcoat?*" my correspondent suggests. "A heavy coat such as soldiers wear when on sentry duty? I have found the word in old Nova Scotia MSS."

OWEN WISTER.

Long House, Bryn Mawr, 1928.

# U. S. GRANT

TO

# M. C. W.

FROM O. W.


*. . . mihi parva rura et
Spiritum Graiae tenuem Camenae
Parca non mendax dedit, et malignum
Spernere vulgus.*

# PREFACE

THIS short book is derived from long ones; from pamphlets, speeches, essays, and newspapers; from certain pages of the official records; and from a few personal memories kindly given by friends of General Grant to the writer. These latter change nothing in the features, but serve to touch up the likeness, of the established portrait. Grant is a large figure to pack in a small box: the task has been one of omission. Those authors to whom the writer is most grateful are Richardson, Fiske, Coppée, Porter, Humphreys, Sherman, Sheridan, Newhall, Rhodes, and Badeau ("Grant in Peace"). The writer will think that he has made his own contribution to the subject if he shall have tempted any reader to become more thoroughly acquainted with it.

O. W.

Philadelphia, August 1, 1900.

# ULYSSES S. GRANT

## I

AT the age of thirty-nine, Grant was an obscure failure in a provincial town. To him and his family, for whom he could not earn needful bread, his father had become a last shelter against the struggle for life. Not all the neighbours knew his face. At the age of forty-three his picture hung in the homes of grateful millions. His name was joined with Washington's. A little while, and we see him step down, amid discordant reproach, from Washington's chair, having helplessly presided over scandal and villainy blacker than the country had thus far witnessed. Next, his private integrity is darkly overcast, and the stroke kills him. But death clears his sky. At the age of sixty-three, Grant died; and the people paused to mourn and honour him devotedly. All the neighbours know his face to-day.

## II

None of our public men have a story so strange as this. It is stranger than Lincoln's. It is very

1

much the strangest of them all. We have been too near the man and his time to see them clear through personal, political, and military feelings, mostly violent. All the people are not dead yet. Nearly all the writers have a case to argue. Sheridan must justify his treatment of Warren. Sherman must bolster up Shiloh. Beauregard must diminish Sidney Johnston. Badeau must belittle Meade, and also the losses in the Wilderness. These are mere instances. The heroes and their biographers all write alike, inevitably moved and biassed by the throb of proximity. Such books are not history. They make inspiring material, when read in each other's light. They are personal reminiscences. History never begins until reminiscence is ended. Even Mr. Ropes, in his championing of Buell the soldier, omits Buell the man. Now Buell, sulking over his wrongs, declined, when invited, to come back and take a command again. He found his dignity more important to him than the Union. Grant, meeting singular injustice after winning Donelson, has such words as these to say: "If my course is not satisfactory, remove me at once. I do not wish to impede in any way the success of our arms." Good authority rates Buell a more military soldier than Grant, and very likely he was. But Buell thought of himself and forgot his country, while Grant thought of his country and forgot himself. Out of this very contrast a bright light falls, and we begin to see Grant. Writing intemperately, his friends explain him as a sort of Napoleon; his enemies, as a dull blunderer, accidentally reaping the glory which other people sowed. These extremes meet in error. We have not produced a Napoleon, and military talents of greater brilliancy than Grant's fought on both sides. Purely as captains, Lee, Jackson, Sherman, Thomas, if not others, are likely to stand higher; while Sheridan during his brief opportunity proved such a thunderbolt that, did history know men by their promise instead of by their fruits, he might outshine the whole company, and rank with Charles of Sweden or Condé.

Yet Grant sits above and apart. Is this accident? Is it accident that at the beginning of a certain four years this middle-aged man should be nobody, and at the end should be the one commander out of all to win and retain the supreme confidence of his government and his people? It has been called accident by some grown-up writers. His own words give the unconscious explanation: "I feel as sure of taking Richmond as I do of dying." Not McClellan, not Meade, not Lincoln himself, not any one at all, had ever been able to feel as sure as that. This utter certainty of the Union's success burned in Grant like a central fire, and, with all his limitations, made his will a great natural force which gravitated simply and irresistibly to its end. Lincoln, beginning to feel it from afar, answered the grave complaints that rose after the carnage of Shiloh: "I can't spare this man: he fights." And presently, during the impatient days of Vicksburg failures, he insists: "I rather like the man. I think we'll try him a little longer." Finally comes the renowned remark, when they tell him of Grant's intemperance: "I wish I knew what brand of whisky he drinks. I would send a barrel to all my other generals." Sherman felt the power near at hand, as he fought under Grant, and wrote to him that it was something which he could liken "to nothing else than the faith a Christian has in his Saviour." Through this faith, then, the obscure man from Galena began in April, 1861, and by April, 1864, was the will-power of his country.

But why was such a man still obscure at the age of thirty-nine? Again his own words give the fundamental explanation: "As I grow older, I become more indolent, my besetting sin through life." This was written in 1873 to his minister to England, and no truer word ever came from him. Together with the remark about taking Richmond, it reveals the foundation upon which the whole man was built. Great will and great indolence met about equally in Grant; therefore he stood still, needing a push from without to move him. The gun that fired on Sumter was the push. Until that day he resembled a large animal hibernating. To what he did and left undone his other qualities contributed; but these two controlled,—indolence and will. In their light his story can be plainly read, his portrait clearly seen.

## III

Various ardent pens have attempted to embellish Grant's boyhood. He has even been given illustrious descent. It is enough to know for certain that, Scotch in blood and American since 1630, he was of the eighth generation, and counted a grandfather in the Revolution, besides other soldier ancestors. The first Grant, Matthew, probably landed at Nantucket, Massachusetts, May 30, 1630. In 1636 he helped establish the town of Windsor, Connecticut. He was its first surveyor and a trusted citizen. Samuel, Solomon, Noah, Adoniram, that is what the Grants in colonial Connecticut were called. And with such names as these they did what all the other colonial Noahs and Adonirams were doing. None of them rose to uncommon dimensions; but they, and such as they, were then, as they are now, the salt and leaven of our country. After the Revolution, as our frontier widened and the salt and leaven began to be sprinkled westward, Captain

Noah Grant went gradually to the Ohio River, leaving there no riches and many children. One of these, Jesse, became a tanner, and in 1821 married Miss Hannah Simpson from Pennsylvania.

On April 27, 1822, at Point Pleasant on the Ohio River, twenty-five miles above Cincinnati, was born their eldest son, and christened Hiram Ulysses,— Hiram because his grandfather liked the name, Ulysses because his step-grandmother had been reading Fénelon. Seventeen years later, when the boy was appointed to the Military Academy, "Mr. Hamer, knowing Mrs. Grant's name was Simpson, and that we had a son named Simpson, somehow got the matter a little mixed up in making the nomination and sent the name in Ulysses S. Grant." Such is the father's narrative. And before leaving Grant's plain, self-reliant, uncommercial ancestry, of which his own character is such a natural and relevant product, let it be noted that Jesse, besides writing good clear prose, not unlike his son's, could turn verses fairly well, and also that a neighbour remarked of Ulysses that he "got his sense from his mother." As to Ulysses and the congressional error in his name, he never succeeded in correcting it. The consequences were that the boy came variously to be known as Lyssus, Lys, Useless, Uncle Sam, and Unconditional Surrender. His whole story is here written in nicknames.

Grant's boyhood is like his ancestry,—wholesome, pastoral, inconspicuous. With a rustic schooling, a love of the woods, a preference for idleness, and an affinity for horse flesh, his recorded words and deeds—save one—might be those not of a thousand, but a million American boys. He repeated "a noun is the name of a thing . . . until I had come to believe it," so he says himself. "When I was seven or eight years of age, I began hauling all the wood used in the house and shops. . . . When about eleven years old, I was strong enough to hold a plough. From that age until seventeen I did all the work done with horses. . . . While still quite young, I had visited Cincinnati, forty-five miles away, several times alone. . . . I did not like to work; but I did as much of it while young as grown men can be hired to do in these days, and attended school at the same time. . . . The rod was freely used there, and I was not exempt from its influence." This steadfast, manly, not bright boy had quiet grey-blue eyes, a strong, straight nose, straight brown hair, and a bulky build. His understanding of horses, and the manner in which he was successfully trusted with them on overnight journeys while still a child, bear witness to the tough fibre of responsibility and courage in him. Nor was he pugnacious, but rather the reverse; and this, too, helps a portrait of the boy from which the features

of the man seem a natural, slow development. It
would be strangely inconsistent to find in Grant's
adolescence any signs of precocity, such as mark,
for example, the early years of Webster, another
rustic boy with very similar antecedents. For intellect was Webster's gift, while character was
Grant's; and character finds no outward expression
save in life's chances. Napoleon owes his fame to
himself, but Wellington owes his fame to Napoleon;
and, save for the Civil War, Grant's force would
have slumbered in him from the cradle to the grave.

Here is the single prophetic incident. It has been
told in many ways; and his own is the best, as
usual:—

"There was a Mr. Ralston . . . who owned a colt
which I very much wanted. My father had offered
twenty dollars for it, but Ralston wanted twenty-
five. I was so anxious to have the colt that . . . my
father yielded, but said twenty dollars was all the
horse was worth, and told me to offer that price.
If it was not accepted, I was to offer twenty-two
and a half, and, if that would not get him, to give
the twenty-five. I at once mounted a horse, and
went for the colt. When I got to Mr. Ralston's
house, I said to him, 'Papa says I may offer you
twenty dollars for the colt, but, if you won't take
that, I am to offer twenty-two and a half; and,
if you won't take that, to give you twenty-five.' "

He was eight when this happened; and when,
after all his vicissitudes, he came to die, the same
native candour and guilelessness, like truth at the
well's bottom, shone unclouded in his heart. No
experience of deceit seems to have cured him of this
inveterate simplicity or warned him that others did
not possess it. "Grant believes every one as honest
as himself," was said of him during later days of
struggle. Is it wonderful that he failed in each
business venture? When he was elected President,
such a combination of firmness and integrity was
an outlook which naturally filled the politicians
with dismay. They could not foresee that it would
prove a door wide open to every dollar which they
plotted to steal. When not far from his end, he
was asked if such and such a thing had not distressed him, and replied, "No, nothing but being
deceived in people." And this sorrowful thought
haunts the preface to his memoirs. Yes, that old
horse story is an omen. It raises laughter, to be
sure; but change the figure of farmer Ralston, getting his undue price through the boy's guilelessness, into Belknap of the Fort Sill and national
cemetery scandals, into Babcock of the whisky
ring, into Jay Gould of Black Friday, into Ferdi-
nand Ward, the final thief who crossed Grant's
credulous path, and the old horse story grows less
mirthful.

His bringing up was evidently strict. Both his talk and life were pure. He seems to have got on without swearing, even in battle,—as extreme a sign of calm force as can be imagined. Even Washington broke out at Monmouth Court-house. Grant's one weakness, drinking, has therefore been the more conspicuous. But in these early days at Georgetown, Ohio (where the family moved soon after his birth), he seems to have been soberer than many in that region. As for an army career, not only had it never entered his head to be a soldier, but he was averse to the notion when suggested to him by this father. "A permanent position in some respectable college," he writes, was his hope, even after entering West Point. "I had no intention of remaining in the army." Indeed, in closely studying Grant's temperament, it almost seems as if he were not, in the last analysis, a soldier, but a patriot compelled to fight. Like poets, the world's great captains are born, not made. The art of war, war for war's sake, struck no spark in Grant. But he brought to its practice a sagacity and a grip of such dimensions as (after some experience) to serve as the equivalents of genius and instruction. This is sometimes cited to point the demagogic moral that education is "un-American." Ben Butler in his book says: "Grant evidently did not get enough of West Point in him to hurt him any. . . .

All the graduates in the higher ranks in their classes never came to anything.'' Now Robert E. Lee graduated second. It took four years and some half-dozen generals to beat him. But Butler's book would be a joke, were it not a stench.

When Grant was near seventeen he told his father that he would never do a day's work at tanning after twenty-one. The sensible Jesse saw no success for him there, if his heart was not in it, and, asking what would he like, was told farming or trading or to get an education. He had no farm to give his son nor money to send him to college, and but a poor opinion of a trader's life on the Mississippi. But West Point offered free education and subsequent honourable service. The father settled the question; and this is the son's account of it: "Ulysses, I believe you are going to receive the appointment.—What appointment? I inquired.—To West Point. I have applied for it.— But I won't go, I said. He said he thought I would; *and I thought so, too, if he did.*'' The Italics are Grant's own, and he seldom uses them. Since his career is offered as an inspiration to American youth, it is a pity that his bringing up so rarely serves as a model for American parents. A sound, sturdy wholesomeness in both father and mother is the assisting cause of most that was admirable in their son. They made no grief over saying good-by.

But across the street a friend and her daughter did; and the boy exclaimed, "Why, you must be sorry I am going. They didn't cry at our house." At that house, however, during a period of the Mexican War when the absent son could not write home, the mother's hair grew grey.

Local opinion of Congressman Hamer's choice was not flattering. "I am astonished that he did not appoint some one with intellect enough to be a credit to the district," said a neighbour to the cadet's father; and no special achievement during those four years of study contradicts this view. The boy graduated twenty-first in a class of thirty-nine, good in mathematics and excellent in horsemanship. But—and here again is the dimly felt moral fibre— he was often umpire in disputes; and he was greatly liked by his friends, who called him Uncle Sam. "Indeed, he was a very uncle-like sort of a youth," writes a comrade, Henry Coppée. "His picture rises before me . . . in the old torn coat, obsolescent leather gig-top, loose riding pantaloons, with spurs buckled over them, going with his clanking sabre to the drill-hall. He exhibited but little enthusiasm in anything." Here is testimony to that mental indolence, or torpor, which pervaded his nature; and he gives more himself. "I rarely read over a lesson the second time. . . . I read all of Bulwer's, . . . Cooper's, Marryat's, Scott's, Washington Irving's works, Lever's, and many others that I do not now remember." His letters home show an appreciation of natural scenery, and this he seems always to have had.

During his furlough at home after two years at the Academy it is narrated by Richardson that, "in accordance with an agreement between himself and classmates to abstain from liquor for a year, he steadily refused to drink with his old friends. The object of the cadets was to strengthen, by their example, one of their number who was falling into bad habits." It has never been narrated that C. F. Smith, the commandant of cadets, sent for the boy once when he was in danger of being dismissed, and told him that he was capable of better things. The words that passed on this occasion have died with the two that spoke them; but Grant loved and honoured Smith with a special feeling, and a great deal lies behind the short sentence in the second chapter of the memoirs. So West Point bears consistent witness to the good and bad in Grant. He left it in 1843, wishing naturally to be a dragoon, but was commissioned brevet second lieutenant in the Fourth Infantry, to which he reported for duty on September 30 at Jefferson Barracks, Missouri.

## IV

He was twenty-one, and five feet seven inches
high, but bulky no longer. A threatening cough had
reduced him to one hundred and seventeen pounds,
—his weight four years earlier, though he had grown
six inches. For a time his hours were fairly free;
and he made the acquaintance of a classmate's sister, Miss Julia Dent, living in the neighbourhood.
When Texas and Mexican affairs called his regiment to Louisiana in the following May, he found
that he regarded Miss Dent as more than an acquaintance; and they became engaged. Before the
end of the month he was in camp near the Red
River on high ground, so healthy that they named
it Camp Salubrity; and presently he was cured of
his cough, and developed a reddish beard that is
described as being much too long for such a youth.
General Richard Taylor, of the Confederacy, remem-
bers him at this time as ''a modest, amiable, but by
no means promising lieutenant in a marching regiment.'' But Taylor could scarcely have held this
estimate after Molino-del-Rey and Chapultepec. In
the months of peace preceding, whether in Louisiana or at Corpus Christi, Grant's thoughts still
saw the goal of a professorship; nor was his heart
in the Mexican War, when it came. He pronounces
it ''unholy,'' and he writes: ''The Southern Rebellion was largely the outgrowth of the Mexican War.

Nations, like individuals, are punished for their transgressions." This forty years' retrospect is consistent with his letter after Cerro Gordo: "You say you would like to hear more about the war. . . . Tell them I am heartily tired of the wars."

On the intellectual side, his letters read stark and bald as time-tables. Mexico, Cortez, Montezuma, are nothing to him. But his constant love of nature leads him to remark and count the strange birds of the country; and he speaks of the beauty of the mountain sides covered with palms which "toss to and fro in the wind like plumes in a helmet." This poetical note rings so strangely in the midst of his even, matter-of-fact words that one wonders, did he not hear some one else say it, and adopt it because he thought it good? It was his habit to do this. It is thus that many years later the famous "bottling up" of Butler came to be so described.

Yet, though his heart was not in this war, he shone in its battles. He was in all fights that he could be in, and in several that he need not have been in. For after the capture of Vera Cruz he was appointed regimental quartermaster; and this position puts an officer in charge of the trains, and furnishes him with a valid reason for staying behind with them. Grant never did, however, but was always in the thick of the action. He was commended in reports, brevetted first lieutenant for

distinguished service at Molino-del-Rey (but deaths
in that battle brought him full first lieutenancy),
and for "acquitting himself most nobly" at Chapultepec he received the brevet of captain. Yet
these honours do not show him so much out of the
common as what quietly happened between him and
General Worth at San Cosme. He had found a
belfry which commanded an important position of
the enemy; and to the top of this he, with a few
men, had managed to get a mountain howitzer.
Presently General Worth observed, and sent a staff
officer for him—Pemberton, of Vicksburg. Worth
"expressed his gratification at the services the howitzer in the church steeple was doing, . . . and
ordered a captain of voltigeurs to report to me with
another howitzer. . . . I could not tell the general
that there was not room enough in the steeple for
another gun, because he probably would have
looked upon such a statement as a contradiction
from a second lieutenant. I took the captain with
me, but did not use the gun." Here in his prompt
and perfect sagacity stands the future Grant quite
plain.

Thus ends this chapter of his life, and in it he
may be said to have hit the mark. His careless
dress and modesty had not entirely hidden the man
beneath them. And now follows a darkening time,
in which he misses the mark altogether. War had

forced him to exert himself. When war stopped, he stopped also. His ease-loving nature furnished no inward ambition to keep him going; and so, in the dead calm of a frontier post, he degenerated. This drifting and stagnation filled thirteen years, but is not long to tell.

In July, 1848, he left Mexico for Mississippi with his regiment. He was a brevet captain, and twenty-six years old. In August he was married. As quartermaster, the regiment's new headquarters at Detroit should have been his post that winter; but a brother officer, ordered to Sackett's Harbor, preferred the gayety of Detroit, and managed—one sees the thing to-day often enough—to have Grant sent to Sackett's Harbor, and himself made acting quartermaster at Detroit. This meanness was righted by General Scott in the spring; and in later days Grant, having the chance to even things with the brother officer, did not take it, but stood his friend. In June, 1851, Sackett's Harbor became regimental headquarters; and Grant was there for twelve months, when he was ordered to the Pacific by way of the Isthmus. On account of her health, Mrs. Grant did not go with him. He passed the next year on the Columbia River, at what is now Fort Vancouver, where he was both post and regimental quartermaster. One last year he spent as captain of F Company, Fourth Infantry, at

Humboldt Bay. Then he left the army, resigning
July 31, 1854.

Such were his moves and removes. Of his doings
the tale is equally brief. He was known for his exploits with horses. Otherwise he was unknown save
to the very few brought by chance or duty into
familiarity with him. To provincial blood and environment he added an extraordinary personal pow-
erlessness to express himself or go through his manners. In fact, he had no manners, which is far
better than having bad ones, to be sure; and a
certain something in him seems to have held even
the most familiar at a distance. But even Georgetown and Galena found him wanting; and this
social dumbness did not wholly wear off until he
had been twice President and had travelled round
the world.

Either great strain or great ennui may drive a
strong, resourceless man to drink; and both at
different times visited Grant, and overcame him.
It has been plainly written, but is seldom remembered, that his head in these days was singularly
light: a strange thing in such a temperament, but
well authenticated. Very little was too much for
him. Never to touch liquor was his only safety.

How he left the army is conflictingly told. He
could scarcely be expected to explain it himself. It
is only the Franklins and the Rousseaus who can be

as impersonally candid as that. Richardson's version closely tallies with what is still reported on the coast. Grant's commandant asked for his resignation, which was not to be forwarded to Washington, but held in escrow, so to speak, that he might pull himself together. He could not, and the plain truth is that he drank himself out of the army.

He departed into an era that was to be one of deepening gloom, remarking, "Whoever hears of me in ten years will hear of a well-to-do old Missouri farmer." Expecting money at San Francisco, he did not get it. Sixteen hundred dollars were also owed him by the post-trader at Vancouver. He saw the man again, but the dollars never. The chief quartermaster of the coast found him penniless and forlorn, and helped him to go East. In New York he was generously helped by Buckner, who had ascended Popocatapetl with him. In the autumn he is seen working as a labourer on his father-in-law's farm near St. Louis. With his own hands he builds a cabin on some of this land, and names it "Hardscrabble." It is recorded that every animal about his farm was a pet. In 1858 he sold his farm at auction. He went into real estate, and next into the custom-house, and was even an auctioneer, it is said. Sometimes army friends came to visit him, for he retained their regard; and, with overalls tucked in his boots, he would dine with them at the

Planter's House. Personally lonely, he was also out
of sympathy with St. Louis politics; and although
the events of the world had at length begun to stir
his strong brains, and he had opinions, not only
about slavery, but also about the Italian war, and
studied maps and newspapers minutely, his com-
ments were received with indulgence; for his audience, looking at the man, could scarcely look for
wisdom from him.

There came a time when he walked the streets,
seeking employment. So painful was it all that
those who knew him preferred to cross the street
rather than meet him. Can any one gauge the despair of a man who, little as he studied himself,
must have known how far below himself he was
living?

In March, 1860, Grant went to weigh leather and
buy hides for his father's branch store in Galena.
He was paid six hundred dollars at first, and later
eight hundred. But this did not support his wife
and four children. He went to the war in debt,
which he paid from his first military savings. In
1866 he refused his inheritance, saying that he had
helped to make none of his father's wealth. This
must be remembered in considering Grant's acceptance of presents in acknowledgment of his military services.

The year at Galena was more than ever isolated.

His quiet judgment, however, seems to have been wide-awake. He went to hear Douglas during the campaign of this year, and, being asked how he liked him, answered, "He is a very able, at least a very smart man." And from having been a Democrat—so far as he was definitely anything political —his change of view dates from this occasion. The words of Douglas caused him to rejoice over Lincoln's election. Except his vote for Buchanan, his single political manifestation previous to this had been to join the Know-Nothings at St. Louis, and attend one meeting. But now he had listened to Douglas, and preferred Lincoln; and South Carolina had seceded. The state of the country became his one thought. It is interesting to reflect that South Carolina, the first state to leave the Union, sent one man in thirty-eight to the Revolution, while Grant's ancestral state, Connecticut, furnished one man in seven, or five times as many. Virginia furnished one in twenty-eight.

## V

On Friday, April 12, 1861, news reached Galena that South Carolina had fired upon Fort Sumter. On Monday came tidings of its capture. On Tuesday there was a town meeting, with a slippery mayor. But two spirits of a different quality spoke out. Washburne said, "Any man who will try to

stir up party prejudices at such a time as this is a
traitor." Rawlins ended his fervent speech, "We
will stand by the flag of our country, and appeal
to the God of battles." These two names must always be joined with Grant's fortunes; and this was
the first night of their common cause. Washburne
in Congress became Grant's good angel against the
public, and Rawlins in Grant's tent was his good
angel against temptation — John A. Rawlins,
farmer, charcoal-burner, self-educated lawyer,
"swarthy, rough-hewn, passionate," as Mr. Grant
writes of him. In later years Grant said, "I always disliked to hear anybody swear except Rawlins." It was over Grant's whisky that many of
these oaths were raised; and, though we have heard
much about the glasses which he drank, we shall
never know the tale of those which he escaped
drinking, thanks to his friend. Grant kept Rawlins
close to him throughout the war, and after it as
long as he lived. His loss was sorrowful and ir-
reparable.

At the end of the town meeting, Grant told his
brother that he thought he ought to go into the
service. On Thursday he found himself chairman
of a meeting to raise volunteers. After his first
few words of embarrassment, he made himself plain
enough. Though an Abolitionist by no means, he
says in a letter to his father-in-law at this time, "In

all this I can see but the doom of slavery." Believing he could better serve his state at Springfield, he declined the captaincy of a volunteer
company, but helped them form and drill, and went
with them to Springfield on the same train. But,
though Washburne's belief in him was already considerable, his influence for a while wrought nothing
in the chaos of intrigues and appointments. As the
French Colonel Szabad vividly describes this period in our country: "Never were commanders of
such high rank created with more rapidity and less
discernment. Those who had some knowledge of
the art of war, as well as those who were ignorant
of its first principles, well-educated and intelligent
men, together with men totally illiterate and vulgar, all received their stars with an equal facility;
and all alike believed themselves capable of leading
to victory." Nor is this a supercilious European
view. When the baggage animals were starving at
Chattanooga, Lincoln complained, "I can make a
brigadier-general any day I like, but these mules
cost $150 apiece." In the vast shuffle and ferment,
then, how should poor, silent, unshowy Grant not
be lost? The marvel is that he was found so soon.
It all seems as casual as fate. Tired of waiting,
though Washburne counselled patience, he was
about to return to Galena, when he was taken into
the adjutant-general's office; and for a while he sat

in a corner, filling blanks with such ease and naturalness that nobody noticed it was well done.
Next he was sent for a few days to Camp Yates
while the commandant was absent. Force was felt
in him here; and he was one of the five officers
appointed to muster in ten regiments at Mattoon.
It was called Camp Grant. But none of this led to
anything. He wrote to his father, "I might have
got the colonelcy of a regiment possibly; but I was
perfectly sick of the political wire-pulling for all
these commissions, and would not engage in it."

While mustering, he had a few idle days to wait,
and, finding himself near St. Louis, waited there.
The town was a pot of conspiracy. Claiborne Jackson, the governor, with a Union mask on, was stealing troops and arms for Secession. Francis Blair
and Nathaniel Lyon, two most competent patriots,
watched him through his mask. At the right moment they captured his entire camp. A rebel flag
which had been flying in St. Louis then came down
to stay down. Grant looked on at this, and presently, entering a street-car, was addressed by a
youth in words that may be dwelt upon. The mouth
of Ireland never uttered a bull more perfect. Secession never drew its own portrait with a
straighter stroke. The profound self-contradiction
between the youth's two sentences has placed him
in history. "Things have come to a damned pretty

pass," said he, "when a free people can't choose
their own flag. Where I came from, if a man dares
to say a word in favour of the Union, we hang him
to a limb of the first tree we come to." In Grant's
reply the spirit of the Union is likewise drawn:
"After all, we are not so intolerant in St. Louis as
we might be. I have not seen a single rebel hung
yet, nor heard of one. There are plenty of them
who ought to be, however."

He next wrote from home to Washington offering
his services, and with some hesitation saying that
he felt himself competent to command a regiment.
No answer came. He went to Cincinnati to see
General McClellan, but, failing twice, gave this up,
too. Of his enforced idleness he writes May 30,
"During the six days I have been at home I have
felt all the time as if a duty was being neglected
that was paramount to any other duty I ever
owed." But now the troops of the Twenty-first Illinois had become insubordinate. It was a regiment
which he had mustered at Mattoon; and it would
appear that the officers, dissatisfied with their
colonel, had spoken to the governor of Grant. The
governor seems to have been puzzled. Meeting a
book-keeper from the Galena store, he said: "What
kind of a man is this Captain Grant? . . . He . . .
declined my offer to recommend him to Washington
for a brigadier-generalship, saying he didn't want

office till he had earned it." And the book-keeper
replied, "Ask him no questions, but simply order
him to duty." On the day when, through a friend's
offices, Grant had received the commission of colonel
of an Ohio regiment, Governor Yates telegraphed
him his appointment as colonel of the Twenty-first
Illinois; and this he chose, and went to Springfield.

There is a story that he was introduced to his
command by two orators, who both burst into eloquence and rhapsodised for some time. His turn
came, and much was expected from him; but his
speech was this: "Men, go to your quarters." They
presently discovered that they had a colonel, although the colonel had no uniform, being obliged
to go home and borrow three hundred dollars to buy
him horse and equipments.

This regiment had volunteered for thirty days;
but, after listening to McClernand's and Logan's
patriotic addresses, Grant relates that they entered
the United States service almost to a man. He does
not say that a month later, in Missouri, when these
same men whom he had severely disciplined heard
that he was likely to be promoted, they requested
to be attached to his command. He wrote his father
this; but he adds that he does not wish it read to
the others, "for I very much dislike speaking of
myself."

His men did not know his feelings as he drew

near what he thought was to be his first engagement. He writes: "As we approached the brow of the hill from which it was expected we would see Harris's camp, and possibly find his men ready to meet us, my heart kept getting higher and higher, until it felt to me as though it was in my throat; . . . but the troops were gone. My heart resumed its place. It occurred to me that Harris had been as much afraid of me as I had been of him. . . . From that event to the close of the war I never experienced trepidation upon confronting an enemy, though I always felt more or less anxiety. . . . The lesson was valuable."

Not much happened to Grant in Missouri; and he took occasion to rub up his tactics. "I do not believe," he says, "that the officers of the regiment ever discovered that I had never studied the tactics that I used." Very likely the officers did not; but at Shiloh the enemy discovered that no earthworks had been thrown up. Somewhat later than this Missouri time a young associate of Grant's, who perhaps plumed himself a little upon his military reading, asked the general something about Jomini's book. Grant replied, with a tinge of impatience, that he had read Jomini without much attention; and then he added: "The art of war is simple enough. Find out where your enemy is. Get at him as soon as you can. Strike at him as hard as you

can and as often as you can, and keep moving on."
In this compact summary speaks the master mind.
But the enemy got at Grant at Shiloh, and a little
Jomini would have helped there. Before the battle
of the Wilderness he is said to have exclaimed to
Meade, "Oh, I never manœuvre!" And it is said
that his library contained not a single military
work. Grant's master mind undoubtedly did learn
as he went on; but, if books had taught him more
of the experience of the world's generals, he would
not have had to acquire so much himself at the cost
of thousands of lives. Sherman's own letter to
Grant, March 10, 1864, hints this, but with the in-
dulgent voice of friendship: "My only points of
doubt were as to your knowledge of grand strategy
and of books of science and history; but I confess
your common sense seems to have supplied all
this." There seems no doubt that Grant possessed
grand strategy—and none that his tactics remained
weak to the end.

Common sense, indeed, was his great weapon;
and with this finally came the power of grasping
a vast conflict of simultaneous facts, and instantly
forming the right judgment of what he must do.
Those who saw him for the first time must have
been amazed to learn the story of the thirteen tor-
pid years. He supervised the rations, the equip-
ment, the transportation. There was not a ma-

terial need or detail that he did not thoroughly foresee and attend to. An officer serving under him wrote back to Galena, "This man is the pure gold." As the stress of experience and responsibility roused him more and more, his brain took in his command like a great multiplication table. From the efficiency of the private as a unit, how much he must eat, how far he could march, what load he could carry, he reckoned and combined, and so knew what aggressive strength he had or should want at any given time, expressed, so to speak, in foot-pounds of soldiers. Upon this material side the Mexican War was a great help to him; and upon quite another side he has the following to say: "All the older officers, who became conspicuous in the Rebellion, I had also served with and known in Mexico. . . . The acquaintance thus formed was of immense service to me in the War of the Rebellion,—I mean what I learned of the characters of those to whom I was afterwards opposed. . . . The natural disposition of most people is to clothe a commander of a large army, whom they do not know, with almost superhuman abilities. A large part of the National Army, for instance, and most of the press of the country, clothed General Lee with just such qualities; but I had known him personally, and knew that he was mortal, and it was just as well that I felt this." At this

early time, however, Grant thought the war would
be of short duration; and Lee was a long way from
his presentiments.

On August 7, 1861, while still in south-eastern
Missouri, he was made brigadier-general, to his own
great surprise. Of his methods of discipline soon
after this appointment a singular story is told. The
command was marching, and food was scarce. A
lieutenant with an advance-guard reached a farm-
house, and, upon informing its mistress that he was
General Grant and was hungry, received a precipitate and copious meal, and went on much com-
forted. Presently Grant himself rode to the same
door, and asked for food. "General Grant has just
left here," he was told, "and has eaten everything." "Umph," said Grant, "everything?" A
pie did remain; and for this the general gave the
woman fifty cents, requesting her to keep it until called for. Riding on to camp, he ordered grand
parade at once; and to the astonished assembly the
acting assistant adjutant-general read the following order: "Lieutenant W. of the Indiana Cavalry,
having on this day eaten everything in Mrs. Sel-
vidge's house, at the crossing of the Ironton and
Pocahontas and Black River and Cape Girardeau
roads, except one pumpkin pie, Lieutenant W. is
hereby ordered to return with an escort of one
hundred cavalry, and eat that pie also." Whether

authentic or not, the story is very like Grant in several ways. The lieutenant could have been with propriety severely punished for personating his commander. This method, however, achieved its purpose thoroughly. On the other hand, it may be doubted if General Lee would have chosen it. There is great difference between native refinement, which Grant had, and good taste, which he had not.

Insubordination, however, whether in men or officers, was neither the only nor the chief trouble which met the new brigadier-general. It was something, moreover, with which he could cope so well that he was steadily gaining, not only the obedience, but the regard of his command. Another thing there was against which he was quite powerless. His wary quartermasterly eye watched a ring of contractors in St. Louis too closely for their convenience. They could do what they liked with the futile Frémont, now in command of the department; but Grant spoiled their plans, and they accordingly revived the story of his drinking. By order of his surgeon he had taken some whisky; and that was the whole of it. But it was enough. General Prentiss, a little jealous about rank, departed from Grant's jurisdiction, saying, "I will not serve under a drunkard." The slander reached Washburne through the newspapers; and he, his faith in Grant already great, but not yet

impregnable as it soon became, wrote to Rawlins.
Rawlins answered, explaining that the surgeon had
prescribed whisky for an attack of ague, and added
that, much as he loved Grant, he loved his country
more, and if at any time, from any cause, he should
see his chief unfit for the position he occupied, he
should deem it his duty to report the fact at once.
"Before mailing the letter," continues Richardson,
"he handed it to Grant. The general, who had suffered keenly from these reports, read it with much
feeling, and said emphatically: 'Yes, that's right,—
exactly right. Send it by all means.' " It is a cred-
itable story to every one except Prentiss and the
contractors; and it reveals Rawlins in a bright
light. No wonder Grant let him swear whenever
he wanted.

For a little while Grant was ordered about hither
and thither in Missouri; but there is nothing de-
cisive to record until, soon after being assigned the
command of the district of South-east Missouri, he
took up his headquarters at Cairo on September 4.

Here he stands upon the threshold of his fame.
So unpretending a figure does he make that a first
sight of him perplexes and discourages each new-
comer. Twelve weeks ago he had been nothing.
Then he was made a colonel. Now he was a brigadier-general of volunteers. One summer had done
this; but it had done as much for half a hundred

others. So here was quite a large company with even chances. But chance and the man are rare comrades. Like many, he had expected this war to be a smaller thing than our campaign in Mexico. That was twenty-six months; its losses, about a thousand lives a month; its cost, one hundred and sixty million. The Rebellion lasted forty-eight months. It was a battle-ground somewhat larger than England, Scotland, Ireland, France, Germany, Spain, and Portugal put together. There were eighteen hundred and eighty-two fights where at least one regiment was engaged, and certain battles where some hundred and fifty thousand men were engaged. The losses in its four years come to seven hundred lives a day. The cost of it was three billion four hundred million, or about two and a half million dollars a day. Mr. Saintsbury, the eminent English critic, has called this a "parochial disturbance." Wolseley, the conspicuous English general, has said that an army of fifty thousand trained soldiers could have ended the matter in six months. But this military man, at that time, had not suppressed the Boers. Such utterances are, of course, merely the voice of English petulance that our house, when divided against itself, did not fall. United, we were a disagreeable competitor for England. Moreover, the Union's triumph might affect England's getting Southern cotton, it was feared;

and in Lord Russell's evasions over the Declaration of Paris, and in the sailing of the *Alabama,* and in the welcome which London gave Benjamin (of Davis's cabinet) when he came there to live after the war, England's hostile undertone to the Union speaks out plainly. We had friends there: the Prince Consort, and through him the Queen; John Bright and the Manchester men. But the rank and file of the aristocracy were full of virtuous rage at our presuming to be a great nation.

No more than Grant does Jefferson Davis seem to have looked for a grave struggle. He and the few leaders, who took the South into Secession, managed to make it believe that "one Southerner was equal to five Yankees." And Davis made a speech in which he announced that he was ready to "drink every drop of blood shed south of Mason and Dixon's line." This line across our country was quite seriously thought by Secessionists to divide all Americans geographically into heroes and cowards. This tribal mania was very naturally heightened by the performances of Generals Butler and Schenck and the rout of Bull Run. In the East the Union cause looked dark enough, when light unexpectedly came from the West. General Grant stands the central figure in that light.

To follow him, a survey of the country must be taken. Through the gallant Lyon and Blair and

Curtis and Pope, Secession presently lost Missouri. This made safe Illinois across the river; for all east from there was Union to the Atlantic. But just south came doubtful Kentucky, and south of that was Confederate Tennessee; and from there to the Gulf and east and west was all Secession. Kentucky, then, was the first point; after that, the great river, the highway whose gates were closed, and which ran between the banks of Secession all the way to New Orleans and the Gulf. Now Kentucky, like Missouri, had loyal citizens, but a Secession governor; and it was the part of the South to secure this state, if possible. But no sooner did General Polk with that aim move upon Columbus on the river, thus threatening Cairo, than Grant secured Cairo himself. The Mississippi was closed from Columbus down. If Polk should get Paducah, the Ohio would be locked up, too. Grant saw this, and, telegraphing the futile Frémont, "I am nearly ready to go to Paducah, and shall start, should not a telegram arrive preventing the movement," waited till night, and went. He took Paducah without firing a gun. Through his prompt sagacity the Ohio was locked against Polk. He now wanted to "keep moving," according to his view of war; but Frémont could not see that Columbus should be taken, and Polk was allowed to fortify there and to send some forces against a Union command in

Missouri. On November 5, Grant wrote to C. F. Smith, who was holding the mouth of the Cumberland, "The principal point to gain is to prevent the enemy from sending a force in the rear of those now out of his command." Accordingly, two days after Grant steamed down the river in the morning upon Belmont on the west bank, and retreated up the river again in the evening. He had surprised and destroyed the enemy's camp; but Polk crossed with re-enforcements from Columbus, and, regaining the field, drove him from it with a loss of five hundred men. Grant was the last on the transport, riding his horse aboard on a plank pushed out for him. In his plain dress, he looked like a private. "There's a Yankee, if you want a shot," said Polk to his men; but they, busy firing at the crowded boats, thought one shabby soldier too poor a mark. Belmont was a defeat, but one of those which are successes, just as there are victories which are failures. It accomplished its object. Polk did not send the troops into Missouri, as he intended: he kept them at hand against further surprises.

Secession's frontier at this time was a slight curve from Columbus eastward and up to Bowling Green, then down to Cumberland Gap. It thus lapped over a little from Tennessee into Kentucky. Its weak point was the hole made in it by two rivers, the Tennessee and Cumberland, crossing it twelve miles

apart. Two forts barred these precious highways—
Henry and Donelson. If these two gates were
locked down, the Union had a clear road to the
heart of the South; for, by the Tennessee, troops
could travel into Alabama, and be fed also. Thus
Secession's frontier could be pushed back; and, as
it receded down along the bank of the Mississippi,
that highway almost inevitably must open. This
was clear to many eyes, but to McClellan's it was
not visible. This general-in-chief could see nothing
beyond his own movements. At St. Louis, Frémont
had been succeeded by a person equally incapable.
General Halleck was the sort of learned soldier who
brings learning into contempt. He was full of
Jomini and empty of all power to master a situation. On him Grant, like others, urged the value of
striking Forts Henry and Donelson. But Halleck,
whether under McClellan's influence or for other
reasons, snubbed him; and so for a while the matter
rested. At length, however, after General Thomas
near Cumberland Gap had knocked the east end of
Secession's frontier southward, and consequently
threatened its middle at Bowling Green, Halleck,
relinquishing his notion that sixty thousand men
were necessary, let Grant go with seventeen thousand, and seven gunboats under Commodore Foote.
This was February 2. In four days, Grant had
Fort Henry. In ten more, Fort Donelson and the

gates to the rivers were open. Secession's frontier
was crashed through from Columbus to Cumberland Gap, and shrank many miles southward. It
was quick and final and Grant had thought of it,
and done it. He was indebted to nobody. His own
letter about it, written to Washburne a month later,
is like him: "I see the credit of attacking the
enemy by the way of the Tennessee and Cumberland is variously attributed. *It is little* to talk
about it being the great wisdom of any general. . . .
General Halleck no doubt thought of this route long
ago, and I am sure I did."

Let it be said that Grant's adversaries helped him
greatly. In dividing his thirty thousand men and
sending but sixteen thousand to Donelson, Sidney
Johnston made a perilous error. In giving the command to Floyd and Pillow, he made the error worse.
Grant knew them. He struck, and won. They de-
serted, leaving Buckner to conduct the surrender.
The news to the Union was a breath of health after
jaded months of sickness. Grant's words, "I propose to move immediately upon your works," and
"unconditional surrender," were like a backbone
appearing in something that had begun to look like
a jelly-fish. He was now made major-general of
volunteers.

This battle, like all his others, has been proved
a mere bungle by hostile critics. The spirit of these

gentlemen can be given to the reader in a word. One of them, after exposing Grant's tactics, exposes his English. ''I propose to move immediately upon your works,'' would be grammar, he says, if ''immediately'' had come at the end.

But now Grant was suddenly relieved of command, and put in arrest! Halleck had not heard from him; and Halleck had heard of his leaving his post and going to Nashville. Grant's enemies, the contractors, had not enjoyed his recent suggestion to Halleck that ''all fraudulent contractors be impressed into the ranks, or, still better, into the gunboat service, where they could have no chance of deserting.'' They therefore had surrounded Halleck with rumours, entirely false, of Grant's drinking. Halleck had had a spy watching Grant's habits in a little house that was his headquarters before the surrender. He now, never waiting to learn the cause of Grant's silence (which was due to interrupted communications) or Grant's reason for going to Nashville (which was to confer with Buell, who had occupied that town), petulantly complained to Washington. It was set right in nine days; but Halleck was afraid to let Grant know the hand he had in it. Grant never vouchsafed a syllable to the world's injurious assaults upon him at this hour or at any other of his life. But in a letter to Washburne he gives us a glimpse into his silent soul.

"There are some things which I wish to say to you in my own vindication, not that I care a straw for what is said individually, but because you have taken so much interest in my welfare." And one evening during the nine days' humiliation, a sword was presented to him by some officers. After their speech and departure, he stood looking at the gift in silence where it lay before him on the table of the gunboat cabin. Suddenly pushing it from him, he exclaimed, "I shall never wear a sword again!" and turned away. Only one or two witnessed this breaking of the real man from the depths of his grief. And generally he managed to keep a face like stone; but, upon the occasion when he learned of his friend McPherson's death, he went into his tent, and wept like a child.

At this time he walked in intimate silence with C. F. Smith, his West Point commandant, and his temporary superior now; and those who saw them say that Grant's manner to Smith was something of an old pupil's respect and something of a plain man's admiration for his more polished and splendid friend, while Smith, on his side, treated Grant as a creature whose larger dimensions he felt and bowed to. Some further pictures of Grant at Donelson show several sides of the man. On the eve of the surrender, Pillow had made a desperate sortie while Grant was conferring with Foote on his gunboat.

For a while it was a bad business; and when Grant
returned, he flushed at the havoc made in his absence: his reputation was at stake. He gathered the
fragments, and before evening knew he was master
by a shrewd inference which has become historic.
The enemy's haversacks held three days' rations.
Others saw in this a preparation for a three days'
fight; but Grant knew it meant, not fight, but flight.
He saw that next morning would give him Donelson.
He wrote to Halleck, "They will surrender to-
morrow," and, when asked if this was not a premature message, referred to the haversacks as the
basis of his conviction.

When the surrender was arranged, one of the
young men—the one who had spoken of Jomini—
hoped that they would have the picturesque formal-
ities of such occasions, the lowered flags and so
forth. But Grant said, emphatically, no. "Why
humiliate a brave enemy?" he inquired. "We've
got them. That is all we want." When the crest-
fallen Buckner capitulated, and Grant found him
penniless in the forlorn place, he remembered Buckner's friendly help when he had been penniless in
New York. "He left the officers of his own army"
(says Buckner in a speech long afterward), "and
followed me, with that modest manner peculiar to
himself, into the shadow, and there tendered me his
purse. It seems to me, Mr. Chairman, that in the

modesty of his nature he was afraid the light would
witness that act of generosity, and sought to hide
it from the world. We can appreciate that, sir.''
Indeed, we can; and we can appreciate Buckner's
own warm heart whenever history gives us a glimpse
of it. When Grant was bidding this world good-by
in patience and suffering, Buckner was one of the
last to visit him, and take his hand.

The pen would linger over Donelson; over Smith's
gallantry that saved the day on the 15th, and his
delightful address to the Iowa volunteers; over
McClernand's good fighting, and over Foote and his
gunboats. About the navy, indeed, a word must be
said. From Fort Henry, which it took unaided, to
the day when Vicksburg fell and the great river
''rolled unvexed to the sea,'' the navy was not only
illustrious and invaluable, but also it made fewer
mistakes than the army. The names of Foote,
Porter, Davis, and Farragut (let Ellett's be added
too) must be spoken together with those of the land
soldiers. As some one has happily said, the army and
the navy were the two shears of the scissors.

From Donelson, Grant stepped into a broadening
labyrinth of action. He wished at once to strike
Polk at Columbus. Halleck prescribed caution; and
Polk, unhindered, escaped south to Corinth, where
under Sidney Johnston the South was massing all
the strength it could bring. Columbus fell to the

Union; and New Madrid and Island No. 10, the next two barriers down the river, were broken by Pope and Foote in March and April. On land it grew plain that somewhere about Corinth the armies must try a big conclusion. This happened not as Grant expected. Restored to command, he had rejoined the army up the Tennessee River, and had approved—wisely, according to many good opinions—the position at Pittsburg Landing in the enemy's country, selected by C. F. Smith. But he looked for no battle just here. And here Sidney Johnston surprised him. On Sunday and Monday, April 6 and 7, was fought the battle of Shiloh, Buell arriving in time to re-enforce Grant for Monday's fight. The words of Buell are the words of an imbittered rival; but they tell the unanswerable truth.

"An army comprising seventy regiments of infantry, twenty battalions of artillery, and a sufficiency of cavalry, lay for two weeks and more in isolated camps, with a river in its rear and a hostile army claimed to be superior in numbers twenty miles distant in its front, while the commander made his headquarters and passed his nights nine miles away on the opposite side of the river. It had no line or order of battle, no defensive works of any sort, no outposts, properly speaking, to give warning or check the advance of an enemy, and no recognised head during the absence of the regular

commander. On a Sunday the hostile force arrived
and formed in order of battle, without detection or
hindrance, within a mile and a half of the un-
guarded army, advanced upon it the next morning,
penetrated its disconnected lines. . . . Of Grant
himself—is nothing to be said? . . . If he could
have done anything in the beginning, he was not
on the ground in time. . . . But he was one of the
many there who would have resisted while resistance
could avail. That is all that can be said, but it is an
honourable record.'' A severe judgment, which
controversy sustains and history will affirm. Inexperience is the honest explanation.

Grant's fame is not helped by covering Shiloh,
and Grant's fame can stand the truth. So also did
Napoleon lose touch of his enemy at Marengo
through failure to use his cavalry for reconnoitring.
He went to sleep expecting no battle in the morning; and in the morning he was surprised and defeated by Melas, as Johnston surprised and defeated
Grant. Re-enforced by Desaix's return in the afternoon, he recovered himself, as Grant, re-enforced
by Buell, recovered himself on the second day. The
Union lost some thirteen thousand men, the South
eleven thousand,—and understood thereafter that
all American blood was equally gallant, whether
Northern or Southern.

Grant made another mistake here; and his rea-

sons for not pursuing the enemy (who had lost
Sidney Johnston the first day) are not convincing.
Mr. John Fiske, quoting Sherman's remark about
it to himself, gives the human clew to this bad military error: "I assure you, my dear fellow, we had
had quite enough of their society for two whole
days, and were only too glad to get rid of them on
any terms." The writer has heard this same explanation from another soldier.

So the enemy, now under Beauregard, fell back
to Corinth, and with needless and pompous caution
was driven from there by the learned Halleck after
some weeks. For the learned Halleck came down
now, and took command personally; and Grant was
again under a cloud, a mere onlooker with the ster-
ile position of second in command. Again, as always,
he answered no word to the furious storm of abuse
which the country let loose upon him. To Washburne he wrote: "I would scorn being my own de-
fender . . . except through the record . . . of all
my official acts. . . . To say that I have not been
distressed . . . would be false. . . . One thing I will
assure you of, however: I cannot be driven from
rendering the best service within my ability to sup-
press the present rebellion." And to his father he
wrote: "You must not expect me to write in my own
defence, nor to permit it from any one about me.
I know that the feeling of the troops under my

command is favourable to me; and, so long as I continue to do my duty faithfully, it will remain so. I
require no defenders.'' Nevertheless, his spirit was
near being broken. He had nothing given him to
do. He was in a sort of disgrace. There seemed no
outlook. Halleck had removed his willing hand
from the plough. At Corinth he had applied for a
thirty days' leave, when Sherman, his good friend,
suspected that all was not well with him. ''I inquired for the general,'' says Sherman, ''and was
shown to his tent, where I found him seated on a
camp-stool, with papers on a rude camp-table. . . .
I inquired if it were true that he was going away.
He said, Yes. I then inquired the reason; and he
said: Sherman, you know. You know that I am in
the way here. I have stood it as long as I can, and
can endure it no longer. . . . I then begged him to
stay, illustrating his case by my own. Before the
battle of Shiloh, I had been cast down by a mere
newspaper assertion. . . . He . . . promised to
wait. . . . Very soon after this . . . I received a
note from him, saying that he . . . would remain.''
Thus did Sherman at the right time stretch his hand
to Grant, and help him rise from Shiloh, and go on
to Vicksburg, Chattanooga, and Appomattox.

As Donelson, so now Corinth opened more gates
down the Mississippi—Fort Pillow and Memphis.
Before the first of May, Farragut and Porter had

taken New Orleans. Vicksburg should have followed
as naturally as the last brick in a tumbling row.
But the learned Halleck was there to save it with
his finical and disastrous meddling. He had a
hundred thousand men reporting for duty: Beauregard had half that number. He had also the moral
impetus of victory, while the South was shaken and
disconcerted by Shiloh and Sidney Johnston's
death. The very brilliant exploits of Mitchell had
opened the way to Chattanooga for him. Mobile
and Vicksburg were but feebly protected. Other
men had gathered these opportunities, which now
slid away like sand through his inanely opened
fingers. He sat cautiously down; sent Buell to re-
pair a railroad, which was promptly torn up; sent
away troops to hold unprofitable points; refused
troops to Farragut, who wished to strike Port Hudson and Vicksburg; forbade Pope to risk a battle on
any consideration; and crowned his whole crass
performance with the words: "I think the enemy
will continue his retreat, which is all I desire."
The enemy immediately strengthened Port Hudson,
Vicksburg, and Chattanooga; and Halleck was made
general-in-chief at Washington! To the blunders
of this time may be added the vast farce of the
legal tender act, when the government, against the
soundest advice and warning, declined to borrow
money at market prices, because this would be

"undignified," and issued instead pieces of paper,
which it told the world were worth a dollar, and
presently enjoyed the dignity of having the world
value at thirty-five cents. There are blunders in
1862 so stultifying as to seem incredible, had we not
seen much the same sort of thing since. But we
were fighting Americans, not Spaniards, then.
Happily, Jefferson Davis made some blunders, too;
and thus Grant had only Pemberton, and not Van
Dorn, to fight at Vicksburg, when the time came.

Upon Halleck's promotion, Grant was put in
command of the armies of the Mississippi and the
Tennessee. The battles of Iuka and Corinth were
fought. By November Grant was once again able to
go on with his interrupted strategy of flanking the
Mississippi. It was not until the following spring
that he walked to his goal with a firm step. In the
months between he was not only hampered by many
external embarrassments, but his own mind had not
come to a final clear determination. The jealousy
of McClernand, the treachery that lost him his base
at Holly Springs, and his own not very sound plan
of co-operating with Sherman on the east bank—
these among other causes helped his first failure.
Then in the winter months his canal-cutting, and
various operations upon both sides of the river, were
defeated by Nature herself. Perhaps he should have
known that land and water were tangled in such a

chaos here that the first chapter of Genesis alone could have straightened them for an army. One sentence from Porter's report of the Yazoo Pass attempt, and what the gunboats had to do in the narrow channels that enmeshed them with vegetation, draws the whole picture of this winter without need of further comment: "I never yet saw vessels so well adapted to knocking down trees, hauling them up by the roots, or demolishing bridges." Yet, perhaps, Grant knew all this very well. His troops were in a wretched watery camp opposite Vicksburg. Disease had heavily visited them. The graves of their late comrades were forever in their sight on the narrow levee. Moreover, the country clamoured for results; and enemies, both military and civil, were pressing Lincoln for Grant's removal. It is recorded that General Thomas arrived at Porter's headquarters with an order to relieve Grant, if it were necessary. Porter told Thomas that he would be tarred and feathered if his mission became known.

Perhaps Grant dug his canals and cut his trees to give his soldiers less time to think of their hardships, and to make an appearance of activity until the high water should subside and permit real activity. His mind was digging, too, deep into the national situation. In silence and independence it reached its own convictions, and then, attentively listening to contrary opinions, disregarded these and pursued its way. And in everything that Grant did, the admirable navy supported him brilliantly. On April 16 it ran the Vicksburg batteries in an hour and forty minutes. In six days the transports followed; and Vicksburg beheld the army that had been sitting in the mud for so many weeks depart, to return presently on its own side of the river with a vengeance.

Grant's arm was at length raised to strike. His first blow glanced at Grand Gulf, the southernmost defence of Vicksburg; but the next day he stood on the east shore, the tall, defended, baffling shore which Secession had called its Gibraltar. To do this, he had had to come down the river to cross at Bruinsburg, some thirty-one miles below Vicksburg. "When this was effected, I felt a degree of relief scarcely ever equalled since," he says. "I was on dry ground on the same side of the river with the enemy."

He now manœuvred to deceive Pemberton, and easily did so. On May 1 he won the battle of Port Gibson. He next made his great decision to cut loose from his base of supplies, *and not inform Halleck until it was too late to stop him*. When Sherman with several others strongly protested against this cutting loose from the base of supplies— the triumphant flash of daring and right judgment

which is Grant's highest claim to purely military
greatness—the general listened, but went on with
his plan. And now, indeed, he raised his arm, and
struck. On May 17 he had Pemberton penned in
Vicksburg, and a telegram from Halleck ordering
him to wait for General Banks! In six days he had
won four battles, prevented Johnston's joining Pemberton, and was now surrounding Vicksburg itself.
After the bloody frontal attack of the 22d (something he owned in later life to have been a mistake),
he settled to a siege. We must remember that Pemberton had made many things easy for him; Pemberton was deceived by his preliminary manœuvres.
Pemberton set about cutting him from his base a
week after he had no base. Pemberton divided his
own strength instead of falling on him with the
whole of it, when his was scattered. Pemberton
ignored all of Johnston's better recommendations,
ending by refusing the advice to let Vicksburg go,
and escape with his army at least. All these follies
had been committed by Pemberton; but we must
also remember that Grant knew Pemberton was the
man to commit them, and fought his campaign
accordingly. And so on July 4, 1863, Vicksburg
surrendered. Pemberton remained seated with his
staff as Grant came up on their veranda. None of
them seem to have been of the mettle that loses
gracefully; but in the words of a gentleman, the

Comte de Paris, "As victory put Grant in a position
to be indifferent to this, he affected not to notice it,
and, addressing Pemberton, asked him how many
rations were needed for his army." Consideration
for people in distress was, after the fact of surrender, his first thought here, as it had been at Donelson. And with the same humane watchfulness, when
he presently discovered a Mississippi steamboat
captain overcharging his men and officers going
home on furlough, he compelled the excess to be
refunded. "I will teach them," he said, "that the
men who have perilled their lives to open the Mississippi River for their benefit cannot be imposed
upon with impunity."

So Pemberton surrendered Vicksburg to Grant
in a sulky temper, and proceeded to write articles
proving Johnston was to blame. On the day before,
the noble and defeated Lee was saying to a Confederate brother, "Never mind, general, all this has
been *my* fault: it is *I* that have lost this fight, and
you must help me out of it the best way you can."
For on the preceding day, July 3, 1863, the Union
had won Gettysburg. On this day of Vicksburg's
surrender, Lee began his retreat. Had two separate
nations been at war, here they would have stopped.
But one piece of a nation was trying to separate
itself from the rest; and the rest had to follow it,
and wholly crush it. This necessity was clearly

seen then by no one so much as by General Grant.
Off in the West by himself, his clear, strong mind
had grasped it; and every blow he struck was to this
end, and every counsel that he gave. The North
began to feel this huge force resting for the moment
on the banks of the now open Mississippi. It looked
away from Virginia, scraped raw with the vain
pendulum of advance and retreat, to Donelson,
Shiloh, Corinth, Vicksburg. Here it saw no pendulum, but an advance as sure, if as slow, as fate.
Therefore, Grant's name began to be spoken with
a different sound. And a Southern newspaper perceived in him the largest threat to Confederate
armies. It called him "the bee which has really
stung our flanks so long."

After Donelson, Grant had written Sherman:
"I feel under many obligations to you for the kind
terms of your letter, and hope that, should an opportunity occur, you will earn for yourself that promotion which you are kind enough to say belongs
to me. I care nothing for promotion, so long as our
armies are successful, and no political appointments
are made." He did not now relish the suggestion of
his being ordered to the Potomac, which first came
to him at this time. He wrote: "My going could
do no possible good. They have there able officers
who have been brought up with that army."

Meanwhile Vicksburg had made him a major-

general in the regular army. Lincoln had written
him his hearty personal thanks, and the cause of the
Union had brightened at home and abroad. The
London *Times* and *Saturday Review* had lately been
quoting the Bible as sanction for slavery; for Eng-
land dearly loves the Bible; but now many voices in
London became sure that slavery was wicked; for
England dearly loves success.

Grant was more pestered than ever now with
Jews and other traders. As he wrote Chase on July
21: "Any trade whatsoever with the rebellious
states is weakening to us. . . . It will be made the
means of supplying the enemy with what they
want." His sound sense, however, could not wholly
prevail against the politicians. One would gladly
dwell upon the story of the cotton, historically
important, and romantic in detail: how—for one
example—a determined and beautiful lady with her
French maid spent some six weeks on board a certain flag-ship, and came triumphant away, bringing
all the cotton she wanted and leaving all the reputation she had; but we must go on to Chattanooga.

Again, as in the preceding year, Grant felt that
one aggressive blow struck should be followed up
by another; and Halleck again rejected the notion.
Once more the gathered army was dispersed on
various errands of secondary importance, and once
more the railroad of last year was solemnly ordered

to be repaired, this time by Sherman. In September a fall from his horse in New Orleans confined Grant to his bed for twenty-one days. While he was still in bed, General Rosecrans, after preliminary success in Tennessee, got himself into the gravest difficulties at the battle of Chickamauga, where, but for the splendid fight that Thomas made the second day, he would certainly have been destroyed by General Bragg. As it was, the Union forces escaped, and retired into Chattanooga. The army could no longer attack. Very soon it could no longer retreat. Order was nowhere, and starvation was approaching. Jefferson Davis visited Bragg during this time, and, looking down from a rock upon the beleaguered, helpless army, felt much natural joy. Like Donelson, like Vicksburg, like Corinth, Chattanooga also was a vital strategic point, a mountain funnel—the only one—through which the South-west could send supplies to Lee.

One coherent plan for relieving the starvation General Rosecrans evidently had; and, to carry it out, he was going to employ Hooker's command, at this time sent to re-enforce him. It involved bridging the Tennessee River, thereby to acquire the use of an approach not commanded by the enemy. To state what geographical precision this plan had reached in the mind of General Rosecrans involves a question of accuracy between his memory and the memory of General W. F. Smith. Both with some acrimony have claimed the glory of thinking of it, and upon this point the official records are not quite specific; but the glory of doing it, and doing it to perfection, is certainly General Smith's. Enough has been said to remind the reader that we are walking here, as everywhere, upon the treacherous embers of controversy.

Twice in September, Grant, still in bed, had sent Rosecrans assistance. On October 10 he received a summons to Cairo, and hobbled off on the same day. From Cairo on the 17th he was ordered to Louisville, and on the way met the Secretary of War, who placed him in command of the newly created Military Division of the Mississippi. Matters were desperate at Chattanooga. Rains had melted the country to mire, and ten thousand horses and mules were dead of hunger. October 19, Rosecrans started with Smith down the river to view the best place for the intended bridge to open a better avenue of supplies. Rosecrans stopped at the hospital. When Smith reported from his inspection of the shore down the river, he found the general relieved by Grant, and Thomas in his place. Next day Grant, still very lame, began his journey from Louisville to Chattanooga. By train, on horseback through the washed-out mountains, and carried in dangerous places because of his injury, he reached Chattanooga the night of the 23d, "wet, dirty, and well," as Dana's literary pen wrote Stanton. And forthwith order began to shape itself from formlessness. Grant's enemies say he had nothing to do with it, that it would have come without him. To this there is a sufficient answer: it did come with him. Guessing what might have been helps history no better than the *post mortem* cures the patient. And, in truth, these critics are preposterous. Earth has not anything more childish than a military man airing a grievance.

That night Grant listened, and asked questions of the officers. These felt that somebody had come among them. He was delighted with the scheme for the new avenue of supplies which General Smith explained to him, and his mind was also filled with plans for aggression. After all these days of passive defence, he must have seemed to Thomas and the rest of that company like the flood-tide after the ebb. Next day he went to see where Smith was going to open the road. That night he wrote leaf after leaf of despatches, brief, forcible, unambiguous, and with scarcely a change of a word or a pause to choose one; for such was his great power in this matter of writing what he had to say. He ordered up Sherman from Corinth where Halleck's railroad-building was delaying that general. He sent reassuring messages to Halleck about Burnside, who was threatened in

East Tennessee. As we think of him during these days, reeling off orders and pulling the scattered shreds of mismanagement together, he seems like a quietly spinning dynamo which, silent and unnoticed, in a small house, supplies the current that drives a great system of moving wheels. At midnight on the 27th General Smith began, and at ten next morning brilliantly finished, his opening of the new road. It was the first stroke of salvation for Chattanooga. That night the enemy under Longstreet fought Hooker on Lookout Mountain to retrieve this loss, but failed. The dynamo continued steadily spinning destruction for Bragg, who now did a foolish thing. He sent twenty thousand men away under Longstreet to attack Burnside. At this, Grant nearly did a foolish thing himself. He ordered an assault. But Thomas saved him from this error. All the while Sherman with his army was coming nearer. Swollen waters and deep walking clogged their struggling march, and the battle was put off for them. At length Bragg from his heights saw them prowling in the heavy country across the river, thought they were going to help Burnside, and forthwith despatched more help to Longstreet.

And now the reader must see the shape of the country. Let him think of a theatre, and stand on the stage, and look at the house. On the stage he is in Chattanooga, with the river and mountains be-

hind him, and Sherman creeping behind them. In
the house sits Bragg all around the balcony. A
valley cuts the balcony in the middle, but Bragg
from both sides commands it as if the horseshoe were
not split. At the right end of the balcony is Lookout
Mountain, like a stage box. The box opposite is the
north end of Missionary Ridge; and the whole left
side of the balcony is part of the same ridge. Bragg
holds them all. His centre is up on the left side of
the balcony: his two wings are the two stage boxes
that look at each other across the valley. He also
holds a position in the middle of the parquet, called
Orchard Knob. The parquet is Chattanooga valley.
To attack Bragg, there is a choice. Go at the centre,
cut him in two, and beat the stage boxes separately,
or get round behind the boxes, and attack both, so
that one cannot go to help the other. But the centre
was a straight climb up into the face of the enemy,
and Grant determined upon the boxes. The left-
hand box, the north end of Missionary Ridge, was
to be the main affair; and Sherman was to conduct
it. He was to creep round and there turn Bragg's
flank, while Hooker was to turn the other flank on
Lookout Mountain. Thus Sherman might cut Bragg
from his base, which lay less than a mile behind that
part of Missionary Ridge. Bragg never suspected
this could happen. Sherman had crept out of sight,
gone to Burnside, he supposed; and the Union

troops seemed to him from his balcony to be thinking of his centre and of Lookout Mountain opposite.
So he did not much fortify the precious north end
of Missionary Ridge. He was doing precisely what
Grant manœuvred for. But Chattanooga is one of
the great battles that melt to a new shape in the very
hands of their sculptors.

On Friday, November 20, a day of heavy falling
rain, Bragg sent word to Grant, "As there may
still be some non-combatants in Chattanooga, I deem
it proper to notify you that prudence would dictate
their early withdrawal." "I did not know what the
intended deception was," says Grant. Meanwhile
no battle could begin until Sherman had wholly
crept round behind that left-hand box—a direful
work in the mud, with a bridge thirteen hundred
and fifty feet long to build, and build noiselessly.
On Sunday a deserter reported that Bragg was
falling back. Perhaps he was going against Burnside himself. If so, he should not get away without
some little trouble at least. Therefore on Monday
the little trouble occurred. Up in his balcony, Bragg
saw going on down in the parquet what he supposed
to be a dress parade of the Union troops. Suddenly
they rushed: the parade blossomed into a sharp
encounter, and before the Southern troops well
knew what it meant they had lost Orchard Knob.
So the Union was a mile nearer to the rising land at

the foot of Missionary Ridge. Bragg showed his
strength on top, and then Grant knew that he was
not retreating. Orchard Knob was now strengthened with artillery. Bragg was frightened, and
took troops away from Lookout Mountain across to
the other side, where the unseen Sherman was
approaching. Through that night Sherman came
out from the concealing hills upon the river,
dropped silently down the river on the bridge-
boats, caught all the rebel river pickets but one, and
by dawn began his noiseless bridge of thirteen
hundred feet, which General Smith finished by noon.
By one, he was marching to the foot of the ridge in
a drizzling rain, hidden by clouds from the enemy's
watch across the theatre on Lookout Mountain.
By this Tuesday night he was upon his end of
Missionary Ridge, and for the first time saw a gap
splitting him from the rest of the ridge. That retarding gap greatly changed the battle's intended
shape. So much for Sherman on Tuesday, on the
left.

On the right, Hooker was unexpectedly strengthened by a part of Sherman's force which the breaking of a bridge had prevented from following
Sherman. Therefore, Grant turned Lookout Mountain into a more serious matter than he had planned.
At the mountain's front, Hooker displayed himself;
and, while he thus occupied the enemy's attention

on top, from behind them a part of his force came
somewhat upon their rear through the drifting fog.
Their picket was taken. From his post of observation on Orchard Knob, Grant saw the enemy coming
down the mountain to oppose the advance there.
But, further round, the other force that had taken
the picket was pressing on and up; and suddenly
the Confederates saw this meeting invasion. They
fired down uselessly. Though men fell in this steep
scramble, the force came on through stones and
thickets, and, joining with the force in front, ascended out of sight into the mist, until Grant could
often only hear the noise of the invisible guns nearer
and nearer the top of the mountain. By night
Hooker was established there.

The Wednesday morning was cold and fine. The
battle's change of shape from its original design was
clear to see. Over on Sherman's side many troops
were now massed against him. Nor on account of
that unexpected gap between the end of the ridge
and its continuation could he achieve his assault
with the necessary celerity. Bragg had taken his
troops from Lookout Mountain to oppose Sherman;
and Bragg, should he see fit, might really get away
without further harm to himself. So Hooker was
ordered across from Lookout Mountain to interrupt
his possible retreat. As Sherman came fighting
along Missionary Ridge from the left, Bragg re-

moved more and more troops from the centre of the
balcony to oppose him, so that up there the enemy's
force was visibly growing thinner in the centre as it
grew thicker on the left. The shape of the battle was
steadily changing. Something must be done to
divert the enemy's increasing blows from Sherman.
Hooker, coming behind them from Lookout Mountain, could do it; but no Hooker was to be seen. His
speed had been checked by a destroyed bridge. He
was on his way, but not at hand for this urgent
hour. As we easily follow a boat race or a game on
land from our arranged benches, so Grant and his
staff from Orchard Knob saw, as it has only once
or twice been seen before, the whole thunderous
pageant, flashing upon the hills of Chattanooga.
And up there, inaccessible to help, Sherman was
fighting the current of a gathering tide. Bragg's
attention must be distracted from him down here,
somehow. And so this battle takes its final unexpected splendid shape, and passes like a great song
into our history. Four of our greatest—Thomas,
Sherman, Sheridan, Grant—stand together in it, the
only time they ever did so,—a gathering of chiefs,
indeed; and with them in their splendour, as is fit,
inspired by them to share their own renown, stands
the American volunteer, reckless at the right time,
suddenly immortal with wild courageous wisdom.
He is told, by way of experiment, to advance to the

base of the hill—that centre which Bragg had been
thinning—and there take Bragg's lowest line of
works. Again he goes steadily, as if on parade, with
flags flying and music playing. Then he swiftly
charges, and next finds himself master of the rifle-
pits, with prisoners captured he has not time to
know how. Here he has been ordered to stop. But
down on his head from the top pours such a stream
of fire that staying is death, while going back is
failure. Twenty thousand of him crouch there,—
twenty thousand bodies, but one white-hot spirit,
transfigured and resistless. Without orders, he rises,
he climbs, he goes on his hands, he mounts the
broken steep slant of hill, leading his captains as
much as they lead him; and the astonished Grant
from Orchard Knob sees him storm the crest and
turn the enemy's guns upon themselves. It is done.
Bragg is split in flying pieces. The stars and stripes
wave upon Missionary Ridge.

When Grant rode up among this seething triumph, the men quickly found him out, and swarmed
upon him by hundreds, embracing his feet and calling his name. And, among all the gifts and tokens
that presently showered upon him for this great
November 25, even brighter than the gold medal
voted by Congress is the memory of that brierwood
cigar-case given him by a poor soldier who made it
with his pocket-knife.

Now he sat in the centre of his nation's bright day. Donelson, Vicksburg, Chattanooga, melted together in his fame. Thanksgiving spread from his deed in widening circles. His message to the government, the pith of modesty, "I believe I am not premature in announcing a complete victory over Bragg," is enough and better than if it had been more. And Lincoln answered, "God bless you all!" And what did Sherman with his men do now? Having "without a moment's rest after a march of over four hundred miles, without sleep for three successive nights," crossed the Tennessee and fought their share of Chattanooga and pursued the enemy out of Tennessee, they "turned more than a hundred and twenty miles north, and compelled Longstreet to raise the siege of Knoxville" where Burnside was. When in a few months Grant was appointed full lieutenant general, under special act of Congress (he was the first since Washington, Winfield Scott being only brevet), he wrote to Sherman: "What I want is to express my thanks to you and McPherson as the men to whom above all others I feel indebted for whatever I have had of success. How far your execution of whatever has been given you to do entitles you to the reward I am receiving, you cannot know as well as I do." And Sherman answered in a spirit equally noble, "You do yourself injustice and us too much honour." In these

letters the two men lay bare their best selves. And
how well Sherman knew his friend! "Now as to the
future," he says, "do not stay in Washington.
Halleck is better qualified than you to stand the
buffets of intrigue and policy. For God's sake and
your country's sake, come out of Washington!"

That is why Grant did come out when he was
general-in-chief. Better, far better, had he never
gone back as president. Assuredly, Sherman knew
him very well.

Ceremonies and crowds attended him after his
arrival in Washington to receive his new rank. His
actual arrival with his little boy was according to
his own inveterate modesty. Unheralded from the
train in the early morning, he waited his turn behind the more pushing travellers, and reached the
hotel book last. Chittenden has told us how the
transfixed hotel clerk changed his manner on reading, "U. S. Grant and son, Galena, Ill." Horace
Porter records Lincoln's cry of welcome that evening. John Sherman writes to his brother the adula-
tions in Washington, and his fear that Grant will be
spoiled. And Grant's remark to Lincoln, "Really,
Mr. President, I have had enough of the show business," completes the picture. No, not quite. One
week later, when he was in Nashville arranging with
Sherman the vast concluding process of the Rebellion, the "show business," in the shape of the

mayor with a rosewood box and a sword, caught him again. Sherman's incomparably brisk pen has drawn the scene: "The mayor rose and in a most dignified way read a finished speech to General Grant, who stood as usual very awkwardly; and the mayor closed his speech by handing him the resolutions of the city council, engrossed on parchment, with a broad ribbon and large seal attached. After the mayor had fulfilled his office so well, General Grant said, 'Mr. Mayor, as I knew that this ceremony was to occur, and as I am not used to speaking, I have written something in reply.' He then began to fumble in his pockets, first his breastcoat pocket, then his pants, vest, etc., and after a considerable delay he pulled out a crumpled piece of common yellow cartridge paper, which he handed to the mayor. When read, his answer was most excellent, —short, concise, and, if delivered, would have been all that the occasion required. I could not help laughing at the scene so characteristic of the man to whom all had turned as the only one to guide the nation in a war that had become painfully critical."

So now he faced the conclusion. From Cairo in 1861 to Chattanooga in 1863 he had marched forward, narrowing the Confederacy blow after blow. Here, between Washington and Richmond—only a hundred miles—blow after blow had narrowed nothing. In April, 1864, they stood as they had started in April, 1861. Richmond was still to be taken, Lee still to be crushed. Three years, six generals, and a loss of one hundred and forty-four thousand men had failed to do this. From such failure Grant received two great inheritances, and with them succeeded. His inheritances were to have his own way unhampered and the control of a perfect instrument, the Army of the Potomac under General Meade. Grant's detractors lay too much stress on the first inheritance. He had his own way, not only because Lincoln had at length learned how disastrous meddling was, but also because Lincoln felt in his marrow that here was a man who would go on and do the thing. He had met no such man till now. He had been looking for one ceaselessly. Upon the Army of the Potomac and General Meade too much stress cannot be laid. Without that engine and pilot the captain would have wrecked his vessel several times. During forty-eight hours around Spottsylvania he essayed direction of the tactics himself, and wrought such havoc that thereafter he allowed the pilot Meade full charge of this.

We may feel sure that Grant underrated Lee at the beginning. He had encountered no such genius in the West. His remark that the Army of the Potomac had never been "fought up its full capacity" indicates that he expected quicker results than he got. And the famous sentence from his letter near

Spottsylvania on May 11, "I propose to fight it out on this line if it takes *all summer*," plainly shows brief anticipations. It took until the following April. And in his own report one reads between the lines something like an apology for these terrible battles. He says: "Whether they might have been better in conception and execution is for the people who mourn the loss of friends fallen, and who have to pay the pecuniary cost, to say. All I can say is that what I have done has been done conscientiously, to the best of my ability, and in what I conceived to be for the best interests of the whole country." His conception was "to hammer continuously . . . until by mere attrition" there should be nothing left of the enemy. He reduced the problem, not to "Who can win the greatest victories?" but to "Who can stand the heaviest losses?" To state it thus was to solve it. It was not military, but it was deeply sagacious. It was like Columbus and the egg. It was also a confession of Lee's superiority. The fact that Lee had the interior lines is not sufficient counterbalance. These awful battles add not to Grant's, but to Lee's reputation.

On his side, Lee evidently underrated Grant. He, too, had been used to other generals—generals who struck a blow and then sat down. But it was never to be like that any more.

There were two ways for Grant to move from the

Potomac on land to Richmond: by the right flank,
westward and inland—an easier country to fight in,
a harder line of communications to cover; by the
left flank, south-eastward, nearer the water—a
harder country, easier communications.

To move immediately south of Richmond by
water and from there cut its supporting railroads
was well enough, provided Lee would keep himself
inside Richmond's fortifications while this was going on. But it was unlikely he would do now what
he had never done before. On the contrary, he
could be expected so to enlarge his circumference
of protection that to envelop him would spread the
army out too thin, and bare its extended flanks to
disadvantageous attack while fighting for possession of the radiating railroads. Moreover, since Lee
had to be bitterly encountered somewhere, it was
better to meet him further from his home and
nearer our own supplies. This, too, for a while
screened Washington.

Grant moved by the left flank May 3, choosing
a midnight start. But Lee saw him before he could
get beyond the unpropitious country, and compelled
a battle May 5.

On that beginning day the two crossed weapons,
both of perfect steel. Lee handled his like a great
swordsman: Grant handled his like a great black-
smith. Lee had some seventy thousand men: Grant,

some one hundred and twenty thousand. Day, and often night, the weapons struck fire at some point; day and night, during not weeks, but months. Some of these clashes have names forever reddened with slaughter,—the Wilderness, Spottsylvania, North Anna, Cold Harbor; but in between them flowed nameless streams of blood continuously. More sublimely shines the American volunteer at Cold Harbor than at Chattanooga,—more sublime in walking calmly to visible death than in tumultuously rushing to victory. He stood in the centre with the enemy in a great half-wheel around him, and, knowing that some one had blundered, walked into this. First he wrote his name and home, and fastened the address to his clothes. Thus they would know whose body it was. Then, at the word, he went. Six thousand Union soldiers were killed at Cold Harbor in one hour. In the book of noble deeds from Thermopylæ down, is there a more heroic page than this?

By November 1 Grant had lost eighty thousand men—more than Lee began with. The army of the Potomac, the weapon of fine temper, was hacked into a saw by the usage it had received. Nor was Lee crushed yet, nor Richmond yet taken. In Grant's pictures the story is plain; the saddened eyes, the worn face, the mouth shut down tight all around. The heavy strain—heavier these months than Lincoln's—with distant campaigns to plan,

near battles to fight, disloyal politics in the North,
and the usual popular imbecile clamour for a
change or a cessation, bore Grant down inwardly.
He carried the Union on his back; and other generals had failed him, and he had been a disappointment to himself. He gave in to drink, it seems, at
times. Discovering this, Ben Butler appears to have
blackmailed him. He had requested Butler's removal for bad conduct at Petersburg. Butler
visited him. He backed down. Not from personal
fear. The Union cause was trembling in politics.
A public tale of drink might remove the general,
and split the Union forever. Presently Sherman's
and Sheridan's successes clinched Lincoln's election. Next Butler showed incompetence again.
Then Grant dismissed him. Butler could have published as much about drink as he pleased. The
Union was safe. Wound up in this, contemporane-
ously rather than logically, is General W. F.
Smith's severe fate. Under first impressions of him
received at Chattanooga, Grant had thought him
worthy a high command, and at this time designed
him for Butler's successor. But in the same twenty-
four hours with Butler's blackmail, General Smith
criticised to Grant's face the battle of Cold Harbor.
Thinking this over, it struck Grant that General
Smith had meant to "whip him over Meade's
shoulder," as he phrased it. He relieved his cam-

paign of so captious a subordinate. It was, perhaps, advisable, but seems harsh.

Yet, if the North was dismayed by Grant's destructive battles, still more so was the South. They felt the end coming. Each bloody crisis saw Grant move on. Such a thing had not been seen before.

Early's almost successful attempt to take Washington did not frighten Grant from his siege of Petersburg. He merely let Sheridan loose upon Early, and broke him. That also settled the Shenandoah Valley, Secession's fertile incubator and truck garden. Sent there during three years to handle it with gloves, our soldiers had seen it so periodically that they called it *Harper's Weekly*. At length Sheridan, though inexcusably brutal in his barn-burning, yet, in destroying crops and forage, merely treated the valley as it should have been treated at first. But Secession considered that Union should fight with gloves. When Union began a fight to a finish, Secession cried out. Sheridan is still denounced; but Secession's massacre of Fort Pillow and burning of Chambersburg are not mentioned.

So the South knew that in Grant's deadly grip and will was something fateful, never met till now. And that grip was seizing it elsewhere. Besides Sheridan, Sherman was closing in upon it in Georgia, and Thomas soon struck it heavily at Nashville.

These simultaneous strides of disaster had all been
set and kept in motion by the single central will.
And, no matter what the impatient country said,
the president stood Grant's friend through thick
and thin. The Secretary of War had made one supreme effort to maintain his dictatorship over the
movements of the army. The report of his fall is
thus: Hearing from Grant that certain troops were
to be disposed in a certain way, he objected that
he had other plans, and could not allow it. Grant
said, "But the order has been given." The domi-
neering Stanton then objected much more; and always, when he paused, Grant imperturbably replied, "But the order has been given." The
Secretary rushed to Lincoln. Lincoln said, "But
Congress has made him general of all the armies."
The Secretary still poured himself out; and still
the deprecating Lincoln murmured only, "But Congress has made him general of all the armies."
There it stopped permanently.

And Lincoln's words to Grant through this time,
though once he expresses a hope that as few lives
as possible may be sacrificed, show his deep faith
and his deep satisfaction in his aggressive, indom-
itable general. In August he writes: "The particu-
lars of your campaign I neither know nor seek to
know. I wish not to intrude any restraints or con-
straints upon you." Grant's reply unites a modesty

and a self-reliance that Lincoln had not heard until this general came. "Should my success be less than I desire or expect, the least I can say is the fault is not yours." No wonder Lincoln liked his new commander! He writes again, when less firm spirits at Washington had been counselling a halt: "I have seen your despatch expressing your unwillingness to break your hold where you are. Neither am I willing. Hold on with a bull-dog grip, and chew and choke as much as possible."

The withers of the South were being wrung. Side failures did nothing to obscure the looming end. The great blows of Sherman, Sheridan, and Thomas sent their shocks to the heart of Secession; and at the heart sat Grant, holding Lee tight in Richmond. It is recorded of his ceaseless work at this period, that on one day he wrote forty-two important despatches.

This winter was a time of thought for the weary, disenchanted Southern people and a time of desperation on the part of their political misleaders. In early February some of these had, in good faith, visited Grant to talk of peace, which talk he had tactfully evaded, while showing them all hospitality at his headquarters. With tact still greater he had persuaded Lincoln to come and see them himself instead of sending Seward as an emissary. But this ended in nothing, save that Grant's character and kindness won the high admiration of the Confederate vice-president, Stephens, who wrote: "He is one of the most remarkable men I ever met. He does not seem to be aware of his powers." Presently again the South asked for a peace talk, this time through General Lee, who addressed Grant in a letter. But Grant explained that terms of peace were not in his province; that his authority allowed him to act only regarding military subjects, such as the exchange of prisoners. And the matter stopped there. Lee's actions and spirit must be kept wide apart from those of the Secession politicians at this time and at all times. Under the inspiration of Jefferson Davis, in the spring a manifesto issued from the Confederate Congress, which struggled to goad the people to further efforts and sacrifices by such prophecies as follow: If the Union won, "not only would the property and estates of vanquished rebels be confiscated, but they would be divided and distributed among our African bondsmen." "Our enemies have threatened to deport our entire white population, and supplant it with a new population drawn from their own territories and from European countries." The manifesto further says: "Failure makes us vassals of an arrogant people. Failure will compel us to drink the cup of humiliation, even to the bitter dregs of having the history of our struggle written

by New England historians.'' But even this ex-
cruciating peril seemed to the Southern people,
whose sons were dead and whose livelihood was
gone, a less calamity than paying a thousand dollars
of their money for a barrel of flour, and seeing their
white-haired fathers and fifteen-year-old boys now
forcibly thrown into the mill of blood. They
wanted peace. They began to see in Jefferson Davis
and his associates, not a group of patriots, but a
heartless, selfish, unscrupulous gang of intriguers.
They began to go home from the army. There was
no pay and no food for those who devotedly remained faithful to Lee. Grant was closing in. On
April 3 Lee had to break cover, and retreat from
Richmond. Davis fled southward; and, even while
flying, and with full knowledge of the crumbling
house, he made another speech, to lure, if possible,
more victims to the slaughter. ''We have now entered upon a new phase of the struggle,'' he said.
''Relieved from the necessity of guarding particular
points, our army will be free to move from point
to point, to strike the enemy in detail far from his
base.''

Few could have believed him. But the soldiers,
ragged and starved, followed and fought under
their beloved Lee across the rainy fields of Virginia.

No successes now changed a muscle of Grant's im-
passive face. Nothing but the capture of prisoners

wakened visible elation in him. Each prisoner
meant one enemy less to fight, one more life saved
from fruitless sacrifice. Of his thoughts, only his
actions show anything. When leaving headquarters at City Point on March 29 for this last struggle, he bade his wife good-by with more than his
daily tenderness, which was always great. He kissed
her again and again at the door, as though their
next meeting might never be, or would not be until
after much had happened. Then Lincoln walked to
the train with him, said, "God bless you all!" with
an unsteady voice, and they moved away to begin
the taking of Richmond. "The President," said
Grant, "is one of the few who have not attempted
to extract from me a knowledge of my movements,
although he is the only one who has a right to
know them."

Rain fell the next day and dulled the army's
spirits, but weather made no change in the quiet
general. And Sheridan rode in through the rain
from his cavalry to headquarters, talked with the
staff and with Grant, and departed to his coming
battles like a meteor, leaving a trail of fired enthusiasm behind him. To this star in these final
days the great wagon of the army seemed hitched.
Whatever they separately did,—and they were doing something during every hour,—the fierce white
light of Sheridan's genius beats upon the whole; and

his deeds against the enemy are like strokes of
lightning. On the morning of April 3 Lincoln came
to Grant in captured Petersburg, and shook his
hand and poured out his thanks a long while. He
said this was something like his expectations, only
that he had imagined Sherman would have been
brought from the South to share in it. Then he
learned more of his general's tact, for Grant told
him it was justice that the army which fought Lee
from the beginning should fight him at the end and
divide the glory with no one. Thus there could be
no rancour. The close partisans of Meade, bitter
over the great slight which history has so far done
his fame, contend that he should have received the
final surrender; but a later generation must think
that this belonged to the general-in-chief. Had
Grant's brooding mind been occupied with any
thoughts save how best to end the matter and how
best to be merciful to the vanquished, he could
scarcely be excused. But he thought neither of
himself nor of any other of the victors. So he and
Lincoln talked together awhile at Petersburg, and
understood each other well; for one thought filled
them both,—leniency. Then Grant went forward,
and learned of Richmond's fall. But no wish to
enter and gloat over his prize was in the conqueror's
heart. As he had asked at Donelson, Why humiliate
a brave enemy? and as at Vicksburg he had for-

bidden a cheer to be raised over the surrendered, or any taunt made as they passed, so now he avoided Richmond; and Lee's last march went on. The good deeds and the exploits of Sheridan's cavalry spurred the infantry to a race. The pursuit quickened; and Sheridan, striking blow on blow at the front, forever called back for greater speed. Lee must not escape to Danville. Lee must be headed off, and compelled to fight again. Newhall, of Sheridan's staff, writes: "All along the road were evidences of the demoralisation of the enemy. Flankers and scouting parties of cavalry were continually bringing in scores of prisoners from the woods on either side,—prisoners who would throw down their arms at the sight of blue uniforms and request to be captured. The steadfast women who begged them to turn back and face us again had been laughed to scorn."

At dark on April 5 word came from Sheridan to Grant: "I wish you were here. I see no escape for General Lee." Grant called for his horse, and rode through the night to Sheridan and Meade. And on the next day at Sailor's Creek the clouds sank lower round Lee. Again Grant's actions reveal his thoughts. On Friday, April 7, he wrote Lee: "The last week must convince you of the hopelessness of further resistance. I regard it as my duty to shift from myself the responsibility of any further effu-

sion of blood by asking of you the surrender of the
army of Northern Virginia." The unsuccessful
battles, the dwindling regiments, the starvation, the
retreat cut off,—all this was plainly the end; and
it stared Lee in the face. But on such a sight Lee
had not at first the moral strength to open his eyes.
The pain was too blinding. In his youth he had
taken an oath to support the government. That government had educated him to be a soldier. He had
been against Secession. But, when the time came to
choose between Secession and his oath, he chose (not
without reluctance) to break his oath, and turn
against the government the teaching it had given
him. And now here he sat, with his lost cause like
a broken idol in his hands. For a moment he shrank
from the final pang of renunciation. "I have received your note," he replied to Grant on that same
Friday. "Though not entertaining the opinion you
express of the hopelessness of further resistance, I
reciprocate your desire to avoid useless effusion of
blood, and therefore ask the terms you will offer."
And Grant on Saturday replied, "Peace being my
great desire, there is but one condition—that the
men and officers surrendered shall be disqualified
for taking up arms until properly exchanged."
And then follows a touch of his perfect consideration for the defeated opponent: "I will meet you
or will designate officers to meet any officers you

may name." So did Washington write to Cornwallis, as Horace Porter reminds us. But Lee would himself go through with whatever had to come. Only still he pushed the bitter cup away from him. "I cannot meet you with a view to surrender," he answered; "but, as far as your proposal may tend to the restoration of peace, I shall be pleased to meet you." And he named Sunday morning, on the old stage-road between the picket lines.

This disappointing word came to Grant in the heart of the night, where he lay sleepless from many hours of pain in his head. Hunger, fatigue, exposure, and strain had brought on such torments that he had allowed remedies to be tried, but without avail. He lay down again. In the early hours he was found walking up and down outside, holding his head with both hands. He now wrote a third time to Lee that he had no authority to treat of peace, but that peace could be had, and lives and property saved, by the South's laying down their arms. An urgency, almost an appeal, pervades this letter. He then declined advice to take an ambulance for the sake of his severe pain, and, mounting once more, proceeded toward Sheridan's front. It was near noon now; and, as he went, a despatch overtook him. Time and further mischances had brought Lee to the point. He requested an interview for the purpose of surrender according to the terms offered. As Grant read and understood that here in his hand at last lay peace, all pain left him. He dismounted, and by the roadside wrote his answer. While he was doing this, and hurrying forward to the meeting, Lee some six miles away lay waiting. Stretched on a blanket under an apple-tree by the road, he contemplated the sunshine that bathed Virginia. Of his thoughts, also, only his actions reveal anything. When Grant's note reached him, he rose, and had soon ridden into Appomattox Court-house, and in a house there waited for Grant. In a little while Grant reached the grassy village street; and there, dismounted, stood Sheridan and others. No significant words were spoken in this hour. Silence is the only reference that men make to great events which they are in the midst of. The ordinary greetings of every day were briefly given. The house where General Lee waited was pointed out to Grant; and he went in, leaving most of the others upon the porch. There they sat, while General Lee's grey horse cropped the grass near them. Quietness was over the little village and the armies lying in the country round. The door opened, and two of those on the porch were signed to come in. They entered, it is said, treading as those do who steal into a sick-chamber, while the rest still sat on the porch. When the door next opened, they rose. For out of it General Lee

came, splendid, tall, grey-bearded, immovable.
They looked at him and his sword and spotless grey
uniform. He stood absently on the step, gazing
away across Virginia; and two or three times he
struck one hand against the other. Then, having
spoken no word, and noticing his grey horse that
had been brought him, he mounted, and rode away.
As he was going, Grant came through the door,
saluted him in silence, and in silence also rode away.
When Lee reached his army, the faithful men
swarmed around him, cheering not their common
misfortune, but the peace that he had made. They
mingled their grief with his, grasping his hands;
and then, almost overcome, he spoke: ''Men, we
have fought through the war together. I have done
the best I could for you.''

What Grant's features concealed on that day we
know now from him: ''What General Lee's feelings
were I do not know. But my own, which had been
quite jubilant on the receipt of his letter, were sad
and depressed. I felt like anything rather than re-
joicing at the downfall of a foe who had fought so
long and valiantly, and had suffered so much for a
cause, though that cause was, I believe, one of the
worst for which a people ever fought, and one for
which there was the least excuse.''

But, inside the house, what had gone on between
the two chiefs? The witnesses watched and moved

always with the hush of a sick-room. And after the first greeting, when they sat down, it became Grant who shrank from the point. He talked to Lee about Mexico and old times, and how good peace was going to be now; and twice Lee had to remind him of the business they had to do. Then Grant wrote, as always, simple and clear words. In the middle, his eye fell upon Lee's beautiful sword; and the chivalric act which it prompted has knighted his own spirit forever. "The surrender," he instantly wrote, "would not embrace the side-arms of the officers, nor their private horses or baggage." When Lee's eyes reached that sentence, his face changed for the first time; and he said, "This will have a very happy effect upon my army." He then told what was new to Grant, that the horses ridden by the men were their own. Again the conqueror's tenderness lifted him into a realm diviner than the renown of victory. He ordered that the men "take the animals home with them to work their little farms." To this nobility Lee's own responded. "This will have the best possible effect upon the men," he said. Moved to greater frankness, he told Grant of his army's hunger; and for this also Grant at once provided. These are the things which the conqueror had done when he came out of the house with unrelaxed countenance, and rode away. As he went, he heard firing from his lines. It was in honour of the news, already spreading. He stopped these salutes at once. "The war is over," he said. "The rebels are our countrymen again."

Thus, when his strength had quelled the four years' storm, did a rainbow rise from his great heart across the heavens of our native land.

## VI

Not even if space were left, should his after days be told. It is not for them that we remember and bless him. The further we recede from him, the more they sink away and leave him shining in his greatness at Appomattox, a hero in a soldier's dress, with sword not drawn, but sheathed. There his figure stands immortal, and there his real life ends. For living is action up to the soul's highest excellence, and many who eat their three meals a day are dead as door-nails. Grant rose to his full height again only when he came to die. As president, he was no more himself than he had been when tanning leather. Men far less worthy have sat more worthily in the White House. It was foretold—silently. Sherman, his dear friend, was set against it, and would not say a word for it. Did he not know the world's great soldiers, and what babies they became as statesmen,—Wellington latest of all? More still, he knew his friend. But we Americans, the most consistently inconsistent people on earth, have passed a century in abusing our army, and in electing every military hero we could get for president: Washington, Jackson, Harrison, Taylor, Grant. When Lincoln was taken from us, no man was so loved as Grant; and, therefore, without asking or caring to know how he could have learned statesmanship, in our gratitude we twice gave him the greatest gift we have.

Before this happened, his straightforward goodness and the power that he had did much to heal the scars of war. Andrew Johnson wanted Lee tried for treason, and Grant stopped it by threatening to resign his commission. In those days the Southern General Taylor writes of him: ''He came frequently to see me, was full of kindness, and anxious to promote my wishes. His action had endeared him to all Southern men. His bearing and conduct at this time were admirable, modest, and generous. He declared his ignorance of and distrust for politics and politicians, with which and whom he intended to have nothing to do.''

Certainly, Johnson did not better Grant's opinion of politicians—nor did those men who now led the South far and wide astray from the noble spirit of Lee at Appomattox. Their continued malignity lost them a great chance, and cost the South dear. Following their manifesto at Richmond, already quoted, they now met each step of clemency with a temper which is completely heralded in the words of Henry A. Wise when he surrendered: "We won't be forgiven. We hate you, and that is the whole of it!" They now, with an arrogance which our language has no word to express, demanded to return to Congress on the old slave ratio. This gave white owners the benefit of their slaves by adding three-fifths of the number of the black non-voting population to the sum of the white voting population. Slaves were free now, but this was the arrangement which the South proposed to continue. Let the reader pause, and take it in. Johnson, for personal reasons, encouraged it, and alarmed Congress. Naturally, the North lost patience; and Grant lost his patience, too. This swept away the Fourteenth Amendment, an admirable device by which any State could deny a vote to a part of its male population *on condition that its representation in Congress was proportionately reduced.* This elastic remedy, which held hope, was destroyed by the precipitate deplorable blunder of the Fifteenth Amendment, the evils of which have stained our soil with increasing blood each year, and developed that barbarism of which the South has had too great a share from the beginning. But, when leaders came to Grant offering him the presidency, either he forgot his opinion of politics, or (and signs point to this) he thought (as another hero has thought since) that being president was an easy matter. None of us can measure such a temptation without having it. As General Taylor writes, "Perhaps none but a divine being can resist such a temptation."

Strange, very strange, is Grant's conduct after his election. He left the world. He went into a sort of retreat at Galena. He would see no party leaders. He ordered no letter sent to him. He would make no speeches. He disclosed his plans to no one. We can only guess his thoughts during this time by his acts following it. They were honest—and helpless. Evidently, he wished to govern without politics, as he had made war without politics. He wished to choose men as he had chosen generals—for their fitness as he judged them. He did not perceive the vast difference: that war at once lays bare a soldier's fitness to the bone, while peace may hide incompetence and dishonesty for many years. As an illustration of Grant's total blindness to the proprieties of civil government, his choosing Mr. Stewart Secretary of the Treasury will serve. He very naturally thought so great a merchant would fill the place well. He appointed him without consulting him. The Senate confirmed the appointment. Then a law was discovered forbidding men in foreign trade to hold this position. Grant asked to have the law changed!

But we will not dwell upon his many impropri-

eties of administration—favouritism, too constant
acceptance of presents, too great obstinacy in forc-
ing his notions, invincible misunderstanding of the
difference between a lieutenant general and a president. It may be said that, when he happened upon
good guides, such as Hamilton Fish, his acts were
wise, as in the *Alabama* case, where he was as right
as Sumner was wrong, or as in his courageous veto
of the inflation bill in 1874. When he listened to
thieves and impostors as in the San Domingo matter, his acts were mistaken and dangerous. And,
alas! unchanged from his childhood innocence revealed in the horse story, he remained such a mark
for thieves and impostors that he came to sit in a
sort of centre of corruption, credulous to the bitter
end. For the end was the bitterest of all.

After his second term, when he had gone round
the world, and met most of the great people in it,
and returned man enough of the world to remark
humourously that at Windsor Queen Victoria had
been too anxious to put him at his ease, and after
his unwilling candidacy for a third term had been
frustrated,—after all his experience, he fell a dupe
to a Wall Street gambler. He became a special
partner. His name was used to further a brazen
scheme of thievery. Into the business he put a hundred thousand dollars, and drew two and three
thousand a month income without wondering how

such returns could be. When the crash came on May 6, 1884, it was inconceivable to the world at first that he was not guilty. Presently by his conduct and statements, by his making over to his creditor, Mr. Vanderbilt, all the property that he owned, and refusing Mr. Vanderbilt's generous attempts to give it back to him, the world recognized his innocence. Help was offered this ex-president who had not now enough money to pay the milkman. Most touchingly, a stranger, Mr. Wood, sent him instantly five hundred dollars, and soon five hundred more, as his share of the nation's debt to him. More elaborate attempts to assist him were begun, but he rejected them. And under the whole shock his body gave way. But his spirit rose. He was asked to write war articles, and presently was able to pay Mr. Wood with the first-fruits of his pen. Then for weeks, sometimes in such torture from the cancer in his throat that drinking water was like swallowing molten lead to him, he fought death away while he wrote his memoirs. The tribute of the country in making him general once more on March 4, 1885, deeply pleased him; but he was shaken by it, and grew worse. Reviving, however, his vast will pushed on with the book, in order to leave something for his wife's support. He had no voice any more, but whispered his dictation, and wrote on days when he was strong enough. He held

death away until the book was finished, and then
gave death leave to come. In June he had been
taken up the Hudson River to Mount McGregor,
near Saratoga, from his New York house. His eyes
followed West Point as the train passed by it. On
July 3 his old friend Buckner, of Donelson, came
affectionately to bid him farewell; and he spoke of
his happiness in the growing harmony between
North and South. On July 9, in a trembling pencil,
he wrote to Mr. Wood: "I am glad to say that,
while there is much unblushing wickedness in this
world, yet there is a compensating generosity and
grandeur of soul. In my case I have not found that
republics are ungrateful, nor are the people." On
July 23 he died. To pay his debts, he had so utterly
stripped himself of all his trophies and possessions
that there was not left a uniform to clothe his body
or a sword to lay upon his coffin. To-day he rests in
his tomb at Riverside. But his greatest visible mon-
ument is the book. Quite apart from its history,
which here and there needs amendment, and quite
independent of its masterly prose, it is a picture of
a noble, modest, great heart.

# CHRONOLOGY

| DATE | EVENTS | AGE |
|---|---|---|
| 1822<br>Apr. 27 | Hiram Ulysses [Ulysses Simpson] Grant was born at Point Pleasant, Clermont County, Ohio . . . . . . . . . . . | |
| 1823 | His family removed to Georgetown, Brown County . . . . . . . . . . . . . | 1 |
| 1839 | Entered West Point . . . . . . . . . | 17 |
| 1843 | Graduated twenty-first in a class of thirty-nine, and reported for duty as brevet second lieutenant, Fourth Infantry, at Jefferson Barracks, near St. Louis . . | 21 |
| 1845<br>Oct. 1 | Full second lieutenant, Seventh Infantry, at Corpus Christi, Texas . . . . . . | 23 |
| 1846<br>May 8 | His first battle, Palo Alto. His second the following day at Resaca de la Palma . | 24 |
| Sept.21-23 | Gallant conduct at Monterey . . . . . | |
| 1847 | | 25 |
| Mar. 29 | Was at Vera Cruz under General Scott . | |
| Apr. 18 | Was in battle of Cerro Gordo, and August 20 in those of San Antonio and Churubusco. Regimental quartermaster . . | |
| Sept. 8 | Brevetted first lieutenant for gallant and meritorious conduct at Molino-del-Rey | |
| Sept.12-13 | Was in battle of Chapultepec . . . . . | |
| Sept. 13 | Brevetted captain for gallant conduct at Chapultepec . . . . . . . . . . . . | |
| Sept. 16 | Full first lieutenant . . . . . . . . . . | |
| 1848 | Married Julia B. Dent, of St. Louis . . . | 26 |
| Aug. 22 | Was stationed at Detroit and Sackett's Harbor . . . . . . . . . . . . . . | |
| 1852 | | 30 |
| June | Ordered to Pacific Coast . . . . . . . . | |

| DATE | EVENTS | AGE |
|---|---|---|
| Sept. | Stationed at Columbia Barracks (Fort Vancouver) . . . . . . . . . . . . | |
| 1853 | | 31 |
| Aug. 5 | Full captain . . . . . . . . . . . . . | |
| Oct. | Stationed at Fort Humboldt . . . . . . | |
| 1854–1861 | Resigned from the army, and was in civil | |
| July 31, 1854 | life first at St. Louis and finally at Galena, Illinois . . . . . . . . . . . . | 32–39 |
| 1861 Apr. 18 | Was made chairman of a meeting at Galena to raise volunteers. Vainly sought a commission in the army until . . . | 39 |
| June 16 | Was appointed colonel of the Twenty-first Illinois Volunteers . . . . . . . . | |
| Aug. 7 | Brigadier-general of volunteers, dating from May 17 . . . . . . . . . . . | |
| Sept. 4 | Occupied Cairo. . . . . . . . . . . . | |
| Sept. 6 | Occupied Paducah . . . . . . . . . . | |
| Nov. 7 | Was defeated at Belmont . . . . . . . | |
| 1862 Feb. 16 | Captured Fort Donelson. Promoted to the grade of major-general of volunteers | 40 |
| Apr. 6–7 | Fought the battle of Shiloh . . . . . . . | |
| Oct. 3–5 | Commanded engagements at Corinth . . | |
| Dec. 20 | His first failure against Vicksburg precipitated by the capture of his base at Holly Springs . . . . . . . . . . . . | |
| 1863 | | 41 |
| Jan. 30 | Assumed command opposite Vicksburg . | |
| Feb.-Apr. | Attempted various routes to invest Vicksburg . . . . . . . . . . . . . . . | |
| Apr. 30 | Crossed to the Vicksburg side of the river | |
| May 1 | Battle of Port Gibson . . . . . . . . . | |
| May 7 | Cut loose from his base of supplies at Grand Gulf . . . . . . . . . . . . | |
| May 12 | Battle of Raymond . . . . . . . . . . . | |
| May 14 | Battle of Jackson . . . . . . . . . . . | |

| DATE | EVENTS | AGE |
|---|---|---|
| May 16 | Battle of Champion's Hill . . . . . . . | |
| May 19 | Vicksburg invested. . . . . . . . . . . | |
| July 4 | Vicksburg surrendered to him. Major-general United States Army . . . . . | |
| Nov.24-25 | Won the battle of Chattanooga . . . . | |
| 1864 | Rank of lieutenant-general revived for | |
| Mar. 2 | him . . . . . . . . . . . . . . . | 42 |
| May 5-6 | Fought Lee in the battle of the Wilderness and . . . . . . . . . . . . . . . | |
| May 8-21 | Battle of Spottsylvania . . . . . . . . | |
| May 23-26 | Battle of North Anna . . . . . . . . . | |
| May 31– | Battle of Cold Harbor . . . . . . . . | |
| June 12 | | |
| July-Nov. | Operations round Petersburg . . . . . | |
| 1865 | | 43 |
| Apr. 1 | Battle of Five Forks . . . . . . . . . | |
| Apr. 3 | Pursued Lee after the fall of Richmond . | |
| Apr. 6 | Battle of Sailor's Creek. . . . . . . . | |
| Apr. 9 | Received Lee's surrender at Appomattox Court-house . . . . . . . . . . . . | |
| 1866 | | 44 |
| July 25 | Rank of general given to him . . . . . | |
| 1867-8 | | 45–46 |
| Aug. 12– | Was Secretary of War *ad interim* . . . . | |
| Jan. 14 | | |
| 1868 | Was unanimously nominated for President | |
| May 19 | at the National Republican Convention in Chicago . . . . . . . . . . . . . | 46 |
| Nov. | Was elected by 214 votes to 80 . . . . . | |
| 1872 | | 50 |
| Sept. 14 | Settlement of the *Alabama* claims . . . . | |
| Nov. | Re-elected President by 300 votes against 66 . . . . . . . . . . . . . . . . | |
| 1877 | Sailed from Philadelphia on his journey | |
| May 17 | round the world . . . . . . . . . . | 55 |

| DATE | EVENTS | AGE |
|---|---|---|
| 1879 | | 57 |
| Dec. 16 | Landed at Philadelphia from his journey | |
| 1883 | | 61 |
| Dec. 24 | Was injured by a fall . . . . . . . . . | |
| 1884 | Failure of the Marine Bank and of Grant | |
| May 6 | & Ward . . . . . . . . . . . . . . | 62 |
| Nov. | Final illness declared itself . . . . . . . | |
| 1885 | Was placed on the retired list with the | |
| Mar. 4 | rank of general . . . . . . . . . . . | 63 |
| July 23 | Ulysses S. Grant died at Mount Mc- | |
| | Gregor, near Saratoga, New York . . | |

# BIBLIOGRAPHY

SINCE even the important Grant literature offers a pilgrimage of reading such as few have leisure to undertake, those books most directly and compactly authentic or remunerative have been marked with a star. Works of controversy are not included. Several volumes, once conspicuous, are omitted because of their present trifling value. It is impracticable to enumerate many documents,—Sumner's speeches, for example,—essential though they be to the student.

I. GRANT AND HIS CAMPAIGNS. By Henry Coppée. (New York, 1866: Charles B. Richardson.) By far the best of the early military biographies.

II. WITH GENERAL SHERIDAN IN LEE'S LAST CAMPAIGN. By a staff officer [F. C. Newhall]. (Philadelphia, 1866: J. B. Lippincott Company.) The most vivid story of the cavalry battles yet told.

III. *PERSONAL HISTORY OF ULYSSES S. GRANT. By Albert D. Richardson. (Hartford, Conn., 1868: American Publishing Company.) Full of anecdote and interest. On the whole, better than either its contemporaries or its followers.

IV. MILITARY HISTORY OF ULYSSES S. GRANT. By Adam Badeau. (New York, 1868–81: D. Appleton & Co.) A pompous third-rate production, and untrustworthy.

97

V. THE VIRGINIA CAMPAIGN OF '64 AND '65. By Andrew
A. Humphreys. (New York, 1883: Charles Scribner's
Sons.) The admirable temper and ability of this book
place it far above any military narrative thus far written
in this country.

VI. *PERSONAL MEMOIRS OF U. S. GRANT. Two volumes.
(New York, 1885–86: Charles L. Webster & Co.; Century
Company, 1895.) This great book has been already
spoken of in the text. With it should be read the Memoirs
of Sherman and Sheridan. They make a trilogy that will
outlast any criticism.

VII. GRANT IN PEACE. By Adam Badeau. (Hartford, Conn.,
1887: S. S. Scranton & Co.) Contains much that is trivial,
but much that is valuable.

VIII. HISTORICAL ESSAYS. By Henry Adams. The four
last essays. (New York, 1891: Charles Scribner's Sons.)
There is no better summary of pertinent political issues.

IX. MR. FISH AND THE ALABAMA CLAIMS. By J. C. B.
Davis. (Boston and New York, 1893: Houghton, Mifflin
& Co.) Another excellent and absorbing summary.

X. THE STORY OF THE CIVIL WAR. By John Codman Ropes.
(New York, 1894–98: G. P. Putnam's Sons.) Unfinished.
The reader may always trust Mr. Ropes's information,
but not always his judgment.

XI. HISTORY OF THE UNITED STATES FROM THE COMPROMISE
OF 1850. Volumes III. and IV. By James Ford Rhodes.
(New York, 1895–99: Harper Brothers.) Unfinished.
This work is steadily taking the features of a classic.
No writer of any period of our history combines so many
gifts,—interest, weight, thoroughness, serenity.

XII. THE HISTORY OF THE LAST QUARTER-CENTURY IN THE
UNITED STATES (1870–95). Volume I. By Elisha Benjamin Andrews. (New York, 1896: Charles Scribner's
Sons.) Entertaining, undigested, readable. A good
cartoon of the period.

XIII. *CAMPAIGNING WITH GRANT. By General Horace Porter, LL.D. (New York, 1897: The Century Company.) An engaging and charming book. Grant's personality is nowhere better drawn.

XIV. A BIRD'S-EYE VIEW OF OUR CIVIL WAR. By Theodore Ayrault Dodge. (Boston and New York, 1897: Houghton, Mifflin & Co.) As a book of quick reference, a table of contents, so to speak, the reader will find this of great help—as did the writer.

XV. BATTLES AND LEADERS OF THE CIVIL WAR. Four volumes. (New York, 1897: The Century Company.) This contains almost everything its title indicates, and is of permanent value.

XVI. *THE MISSISSIPPI VALLEY IN THE CIVIL WAR. By John Fiske. (Boston and New York, 1900: Houghton, Mifflin & Co.) This is an essential book to read, and as delightful as it is necessary.

# THE SEVEN AGES OF
# WASHINGTON

TO

# S. B. W.

FROM HER SON


> . . . *mihi parva rura et*
> *Spiritum Graiae tenuem Camenae*
> *Parca non mendax dedit, et malignum*
> *Spernere vulgus.*

# PREFACE

TO an invitation from the University of Pennsylvania this book is due. The Washington orator chosen for 1907 found himself at a late hour compelled to renounce his task, and this honor fell from him upon me. Saving its scheme, little of the speech remains; English meant for the ear of an audience differs in fibre from English meant for the eye of a reader; besides this, the limit of an address shuts out much that belongs to the subject. I had hoped to write this book short enough to be read in one comfortable sitting; such brevity has proved beyond my skill. I have attempted a full-length portrait of Washington, with enough of his times to see him clearly against; for this, his own writings, so admirably edited by Mr. Worthington Chauncey Ford in fourteen volumes, are the material. My other authorities are noted in a table at the end. Certain anecdotes, not before given to the public, are due to the kindness of friends and to some privately published memoirs. Many things that must have been in his letters to his wife, discreetly destroyed, we shall never know.

Philadelphia, October 20, 1907.

# THE SEVEN AGES OF WASHINGTON

O
N the 22d of February, 1792, Congress was sitting in Philadelphia, and to many came the impulse to congratulate the President upon this, his sixty-first birthday; therefore a motion was made to adjourn for half an hour, that this civility might be paid. The motion was bitterly opposed, as smacking of idolatry and as leaning toward monarchy. Then it was the eighteenth century, it is the twentieth now; but when the 22d of February comes, the United States of America adjourn for a day to honour the memory of George Washington.

At the present time it is odd to recognize that what did come to suffer by the idolatry so much feared by Congress, was not our republic, but the natural, manly, and human character of Washington in the hands of his early biographers. What was done, for instance, to his letters in the generation of our grandfathers, we grandsons would refuse to believe, were we merely told such a story;

but to-day we can look at the original letters with our own eyes, and see the strange tricks that were played with them by their first editor.

Washington wrote: "Our rascally privateersmen go on at the old rate;" "rascally" was taken out in the printing as a word indecorous for the father of his country to be seen using.

In another place: "Such a dearth of spirit pray God I may never witness again," becomes, "Such a dearth of spirit pray God's mercy I may never witness again."

In still a third (the subject is a contemplated appropriation): "One hundred thousand dollars will be but a flea-bite," is changed to, "One hundred thousand dollars will be totally inadequate."

By such devices was a frozen image of George Washington held up for Americans to admire, rigid with congealed virtue, ungenial, unreal, to whom from our school-days up we have been paying a sincere and respectful regard, but a regard without interest, sympathy, heart—or indeed, belief. It thrills a true American to the marrow to learn at last that this far-off figure, this George Washington, this man of patriotic splendor, the captain and saviour of our Revolution, the self-sacrificing, devoted President, was a man also with a hearty laugh, with a love of the theatre, with a white-hot temper, who when roused could (for example) de-

clare of Edmund Randolph: "A damneder scoun-
drel God Almighty never permitted to disgrace
humanity."

The unfreezing of Washington was begun by
Irving, but was in that day a venture so new and
startling that Irving, gentleman and scholar, went
at it gingerly and with many inferential depreca-
tions. His hand, however, first broke the ice, and
to-day we can see the live and human Washington,
full length. He does not lose an inch by it, and we
gain a progenitor of flesh and blood.

Between all great men there is one signal family
likeness; so much is in them, such volume and
variety, that by choosing this and leaving out that,
portraits almost conflicting could be made of the
same character, each based wholly upon fact, yet
not all the facts, and so a false picture of the man.
From Julius Caesar could be drawn a profligate and
fashionable idler, rather vain of the verses which it
was his desultory pleasure to compose. Out of Napoleon could be made a beneficent law-giver, warmly
concerned with questions of education. To read the
several journals that Washington wrote at Mount
Vernon, you would scarce guess that public life
engaged a moment of his thought, or that he had
ever seen a day's fighting. The hints of greatness
in those pages are a huge energy, and a grasp of
detail, a memory and attention for the smallest as

well as the largest things, that leave one silent with
wonder. But no direct sign of the soldier or states-
man is there; the writer is apparently a breeder
of horses, dogs, and sheep, a planter of trees and
crops, generous to his relations and relations-in-law,
with his slaves both humane and strict, most strict
in his business duties to others, and in their business
duties to him. He is also a constant sportsman, fox-
hunter, and host, who is pleased to bid many welcome at his table, but dearly likes chosen friends to
come in; and with these he takes a more familiar
glass of Madeira. To the matter of wine he gives
the same measured, minute attention that he gives
to his fields, his horses, his rams, and all else. Twice
he writes explicit directions about it, the second being as follows, in 1794, when his duties as President
keep him absent from home :—

"In a letter from Mrs. Fanny Washington . . .
she mentions, that since I left Mount Vernon she
has given out four dozen and eight bottles of wine
. . . I am led by it to observe, that it is not my
intention that it should be given to every one who
may incline to make a convenience of the house in
travelling, or who may be induced to visit it from
motives of curiosity. There are but three descriptions of people to whom I think it ought to be given :
first, my *particular* and intimate acquaintance, in
case business should call them there, such for instance as Doctor Craik, 2dly, some of the *most* re-

spectable foreigners who may, perchance, be in
Alexandria or the federal city; and be either
brought down, or introduced by letter, from some
of my particular acquaintance as before mentioned;
or thirdly, to persons of some distinction (such as
members of Congress, &c.) who may be travelling
through the country from North to South, or from
South to North . . . Unless some caution of this
sort governs, I should be run to an expense as
improper as it would be considerable;—for the duty
upon Madeira wine makes it one of the most expensive liquors that is now used, while my stock of it
is small, and old wine (of which that is) is not to
be had upon any terms: for which reason, and for
the limited purposes already mentioned, I had
rather you would provide claret, or other wine on
which the duty is not so high, than to use my
Madeira, unless it be on very extraordinary occasions. I have no objection to any sober, or orderly
person's gratifying their curiosity in viewing the
buildings, gardens, &c., about Mt. Vernon; but it
is only to such persons as I have described that I
ought to be run to any expense on account of these
visits of curiosity, beyond common civility and
hospitality. No gentleman who has a proper respect
for his own character (except relations and intimates) would use the house in my absence for the
sake of conveniency. . . ."

Such orders are given about every item of his

domestic and agricultural establishment, and this all through a period when his mind was deep in public matters of a most vexing and delicate kind, both at home and abroad; when he was writing long letters to Hamilton, to Jay, to Adams, to Congress, about our threatened relations with England, and the Pennsylvania Whiskey Rebellion. Nor were these letters dictated—they were in addition to those dictated; nor yet were they thin or of hasty judgment; they were as thorough as what he writes about his wine; and this radiation of energy and sagacity began with him before he was twenty, and continued during some forty-seven years until his death. Not seldom, in reading Washington's correspondence, one pauses simply to dwell upon the marvel of how such power for work ever got itself into one human body. He judged himself well (his judgment was seldom wrong about anything) when in early life he wrote Governor Dinwiddie: "I have a constitution hardy enough to encounter and undergo the most severe trials, and I flatter myself resolution to face what any man dares."

With the many documents now come to light and a proper study and use of these, there could be readily made (if but words were painters' brushes and facts were colours) a gallery of portraits, each of Washington, and all faithful likenesses. His

schoolboy face might then be seen, and how he
looked in adolescence, when he was surveying for
Lord Fairfax, and between whiles making love so
precocious, continued, and apparently barren of reward. That older face which Stuart has given us,
weather-beaten, war-beaten, deeply toned with retrospect, tells not of those far early Virginia days.
And in truth, to sum up a man as he ends, or as
he begins, or at any single hour of his life, is to
present but a fragment of him; for he is ceasing
to be some things, while he is beginning to be other
things; and it is all a ceasing, and a beginning, and
an overlapping. Who could tell in August what
the fruit tree was in May?

In the October of his days, Washington writes
from Mt. Vernon: ''The more I am acquainted with
agricultural affairs, the better I am pleased with
them.'' And in the November of his days: ''To
make and sell a little flour . . . and to amuse myself in . . . rural pursuits, will constitute my employment . . . If also I could now and then meet
the friends I esteem, it would fill the measure. . . .'' Thus the Autumnal Washington; but
when he was only April-old, he wrote: ''My feelings are strongly bent to arms.'' And again: ''I
heard the bullets whistle, and, believe me, there is
something charming in the sound.'' In later years,
he remarked, ''If I said so, it was when I was

young." The man himself had forgotten an earlier
aspect of himself. Little, then, shall others understand of him who know only Washington the General, or Washington the President.

Life plants no new seeds in a man, but the sun
and the snow of the years both quicken and kill
what seeds were in him at his birth, and thus the
main trunk of character slowly grows. No more
than Rome was the Commander-in-Chief of our
Revolution built in a day; to stand that strain
required beams and rafters of long seasoning, and
if ever a character got long seasoning, it was George
Washington's. To survey his sixty-seven years, it
seems as if so much had never happened to any
other man; certainly no American's life has been
more crowded with extreme events—action and reflection galloping abreast through cities and wilder-
nesses, battles and councils, dealing with a motley
throng of foreign noblemen, native neighbours,
wrangling statesmen, starving soldiers, Indian
chiefs, and negro slaves.

"If I said that bullets had a charming sound, it
was when I was young." Yes, when he was young;
before the pitiful slaughter at Long Island, where
he wrung his hands, saying, "Good God, what brave
fellows I must this day lose;" and before he had
learned to love the sound of the wind in his trees
at Mount Vernon—in short before the sun and snow

had much beaten upon him, and while the beams
and rafters were still unseasoned. Therefore, to
draw as near him as we may across Time's wide
silence, let our eyes travel back through the battles
and councils, the foreign noblemen and starving
soldiers, to his beginning.

# I

When we look among George Washington's fore-
fathers—which somewhat late research has made
easy, though it has not cleared every point—we see
that he was like them, carried on their deeds and
natures in himself, was less a surprise and departure in the family type than many a famous man
has been; and this because his greatness lay in character. It is when genius steps in to procreation that
the bird is of unaccountable feather, as in the case
of Shakespeare. But we find Washington plain
enough in his English ancestors. He came of good
blood, county blood, blood that had fought and
flowed for its king, had preached for its king, had
been to college, that, in short, knew something of
wars and something of books; that was allied with
other good blood of England, not the greatest, nor
yet the least; that bore a coat-of-arms, which, un-
translated from its quaint language, reads thus: Ar-
gent, two bars and in chief three mullets Gules. And
among those who graced this coat-of-arms we find

soldiers, knighted for gallantry in battle, and a preacher, who for sticking to his principles got into much trouble with the Roundheads.

So there stand the ancestors: some with swords and some in gowns; behind them, the fields of England with battle smoke and fair towers, and the painted shields of heraldry.

Such was the boy's ancestral stuff, from such loins did he spring, through an emigrant great-grandfather known in Virginia as Colonel John Washington, a public man, a man of circumstance. His seed did not fall away; the family held its high position, so that seventy-six years after the emigrant's coming, came his great-grandson George into a world where an established place, a respected name, and important friends were his inheritance at birth. With him, a good environment took up and fostered a good heredity: the happiest condition that can befall a new-born creature. Once on his legs, and his own master, the boy made himself worthy of his advantages, and coming from something, became more,—unlike much present-day American youth, who, coming from something, are nothing. But let us carefully remember that George Washington's advantages were no disadvantage to him; it is not ill to dwell on this. There is no harm in going from the tow-path to the White House; the point is what you do when you get there. Spread-eagle eloquence is apt to proclaim somewhat

lopsided generalizations on this head, as if obscurity
and poverty were virtues in themselves, and good
descent and good up-bringing were crimes. There is
nothing in all that, save hurtful imbecility; the
truth being, that it is not bad to come from silk
purses unless you turn out a sow's ear yourself, nor
yet bad to come from sow's ears if you turn into a
silk purse yourself; but it would be a pity if the
sow's ear became the symbol of our Republic.

Let it be once more said (for it is of great interest,
and has been by historians and biographers but
scantily dwelt upon) that Washington was no mete-
oric phenomenon falling into a family unheralded
from the sky, but very much the reverse, a consistent continuance of the family pattern, precisely
the kind of crop (only greater in size) to be expected
from former harvests; soldiers who are knighted for
valor, preachers who stick to their principles, come
what may,—are not such precedents the very ele-
ments and fibre of George Washington? He was
their obvious, proper child, moulded large at birth;
and into his strong grasp was put a great opportunity. In this coincidence lies the simple explanation of the man.

## II

In 1657 began the American Washingtons, when
two brothers, John and Lawrence, came to Virginia
and established themselves between the Potomac

and Rappahannock rivers, by Pope's creek. John
became Colonel John in wars against the Indians,
as, through similar wars in his turn, did his great-
grandson George become Colonel George. In 1694
was born Augustine Washington, who became Captain Augustine, and was twice married. To him by
his second venture (as he styles Mary Ball in his
will) was born George at the family homestead in
Westmoreland county, on February 11, 1731, O. S.,
or February 22, 1732, by our present calendar. The
child's earliest associations, however, were not here,
but with the spot of his dearest and latest; for his
parents, before he could form memories, had gone
to live at their farm on the Potomac. Some ten
years later the house, as we partly know it to-day,
was built by George's elder half-brother Lawrence,
whose inheritance it was, and who named it Mount
Vernon from Admiral Vernon, with whom he had
served as an officer at Carthagena. When the boy
was eleven, Augustine his father died, and he went
back to his birthplace, "Wakefield," where he lived
with his half-brother Augustine until he was thirteen, going then to live with his mother near Fredericksburg. In these young days, when he and his
mother lived in straitened circumstances (the bulk
of the estate being left to his half-brothers), Mary
Washington seems to have been a very admirable, if
not intellectual, parent for her son, beginning well

the training of his character. In later days, her change of disposition and her conduct regarding money caused him pain and mortification. In certain of his letters to her, always beginning "Honored Madam" according to the custom of their time, the language contains (and not wholly conceals) the struggle between the man's displeasure and the son's natural respect and affection. Some of their paragraphs make distressing reading, and we turn away, leaving them unquoted.

No more than about the boy's ancestors need we make any guesses about the boy. Though myths of which he is the hero are plentiful, and facts are few, these facts are strong in vividness and go far to drawing a distinct picture of him, and to giving it definite color as well. We had best not make too much, separately, of the rather uncertain legends concerning his deeds of strength, his taming of wild colts, his long throws, his high climbs; he was evidently well muscled from the first—though somewhat lank and hollow chested, and with no ruddiness of face—and the value of the legends is not their individual authenticity, but their united testimony. Inappropriate anecdotes about anybody never survive: a saying attributed to Franklin will be canny, not dull; a story attributed to Lincoln will be humorous, not stupid; and it is sure that Washington as a boy possessed a body strong and energetic beyond the common, and that he gave much attention to its exercise.

In children's games he seems to have shared like any other child, and that he played soldier and marshalled and drilled his playmates need scarce be counted a prophetic sign, even though it was he who mostly took the part of commander. He had seen his half-brother Lawrence making ready for real wars; to imitate was inevitable, and military sports have been frequent among generations of children who never came to fame either as soldiers or civilians. If we are looking for portents thus early, there is something more in the fact that a few years later, at the school in Fredericksburg, when the boy had become perhaps fourteen or fifteen, his schoolmates would come in from the playground with disputes for him to settle. They made the studious boy, solitary with his tasks indoors, their habitual umpire. In such a boy we may warrantably see the father of the man who fifty years later was often umpire between two members of his cabinet, and once wrote: "I have a great, a sincere regard and esteem for you both: and ardently wish that some line could be worked out by which both of you should walk."

But why had the boy with the strong, well-exercised body become solitary indoors at this time? His growing character might possibly have kept him

apart, but not indoors, and there is another reason
which dispenses with surmise. The means left his
mother and her family of five living children was
slender, and upon the young shoulders of George,
the eldest had already fallen their burden of pro-
viding for himself and for them. One advantage
common in that day to the sons of well-to-do Virginians did not fall to him, the eldest of the second
family, but to his half-brother Lawrence, the eldest
of the first marriage. Lawrence was sent to "finish
his education" in England, but George had to renounce the luxury of "finishing" even at home, at
William and Mary College, and to make ready by the
readiest means to become the support of his mother
and her children. Hence the indoor study, hence the
solitude, both so marked as to have made an im-
pression handed down by his schoolmate, Lewis
Willis. In the manuscript of this gentleman's son,
Colonel Byrd Willis, is the following passage about
Washington: "My father . . . spoke of the General's industry and assiduity at school as very
remarkable. Whilst his brother and other boys at
playtime were at bandy and other games, he was
behind the door ciphering. But one youthful ebulli-
tion is handed down while at that school, and that
was romping with one of the largest girls; this
was so unusual that it excited no little comment
among the other lads."

And now, since portents when they are real are of the deepest significance, we do indeed come upon something worth more than a passing mention. To the boy making ready to support his mother, and denied the "finishing" of college at home or travel in England, fell a timely piece of good fortune: he received the "finishing" from an unexpected quarter; he came under the influence of a civilization more finely civilized than England's, more courteous, more restrained than eighteenth-century England knew.

To any one familiar with Washington manuscripts, that earliest, the school copy-book of 1745, is well known. In spite of its somewhat damaged state, it reveals faithfully and fully that steadfast indoor ciphering which was to prepare him for supporting his mother. The various formal documents of business and book-keeping appear there, copied slowly in his boyish hand for the sake of securely mastering them, and here and there amid these careful transcriptions, a few scrawled pictures of those he sat in school with, and of birds of uncertain species. But even this evidence of whence began that habit and extraordinary power of method in practical affairs, which later served his country and himself so well,—even this is of secondary interest to the 110 rules of civility, also to be seen in this copy-book of 1745, written with more

signs of haste than the transcribed bonds and receipts, as if from dictation. With these rules the
boy's strong-built, rough, and passionate nature
was deeply instilled before he stepped forth upon
his adventurous journey in the world. The part
they played in his life—since his public and private
acts show their spirit and teaching at every turn—
was of the first importance, not to him alone, but
also to his country. Moncure D. Conway, who has
traced delightfully and admirably the French origin
and remarkable history of these rules, says regarding their influence upon Washington's character:
"In the hand of that man of strong brain and
powerful passions once lay the destiny of the New
World,—in a sense, human destiny. But for his
possession of the humility and self-discipline under-
lying his Rules of Civility, the ambitious politicians
of the United States might to-day be popularly held
to a much lower standard." And to this it should
be added, that from these rules and their moulding
of Washington's character flowed his power of address—the consideration and the simplicity—which
won for him, as it won for no other of his time, the
esteem and devotion of those who could help our
Revolution in the direst hours of its need. It is
scarce worth observing that the coincidence of good
seed and good soil is always necessary, and that if
Washington's character had not been the field, the

rules would have been less fruitful. But it is well
worth observing that they produced some fruit in
two fairly barren characters: Madison and Monroe
were also taught their good manners, and almost
certainly by these same rules, at the Fredericksburg
school, and Madison and Monroe, when examined
close, have little to show but their courtesy,
both being models equally of urbanity and incompetence.

It was once supposed that Washington was himself the boy author of these rules; but they date
from 1595 and before his day had known several
translations, imitations, and plagiarisms, among
which was an English version of 1640 entitled,
"Youth's Behaviour, or Decency in Conversation
amongst men. Composed in French by grave persons for the Use and benefit of their youth. Now
newly translated into English by Francis Hawkins." It is possible, as Mr. Conway shows, that what
we find in the copy-book of 1745 was the result of
Washington's reading and amending Hawkins by
himself. But the amendments seem too skilful for
the boy of fourteen, and Mr. Conway's own theory
seems almost a proven case. In 1729 there sailed to
Virginia with his bride the Rev. James Marye. This
gentleman had been educated for the priesthood,
and thus must inevitably have met the rules, which
were a manual among the religious colleges of

France. But he became a Huguenot, and hence an emigrant, settling at first in King William Parish. In 1735 he was called to St. George's, Fredericksburg, where he set up a school, created a large congregation, and died in 1767. To his school went many eminent Virginians, besides those already named, and the good manners of several generations of boys brought James Marye and his school into high respect and reputation, for he taught civility as a branch of education, as he taught arithmetic. As the rules in the copy-book show a correspondence with Hawkins sometimes, but more often with the original French, and as Washington's handwriting here gives signs of haste and correction that do not elsewhere appear, it points to the conclusion that the maxims were dictated to his boys by James Marye, who availed himself, now of Hawkins, and again (and more often) of the original treatise that emanated from the *pensionnaires* of the College of La Flèche in 1595, with the title *Bienséance de la Conversation entre les Hommes*. Let us remember with gratitude and regard the Huguenot emigrant, an exile because of his high principles, who brought these principles to benefit our shores, and became the founder of an honorable family, and the wise teacher of American youth.

For the interest of it, we cite three parallel versions of one of these maxims:—

Washington's copy-book, 20th Rule. "The Gestures of the Body must be Suited to the discourse you are upon."

Hawkins 1. 30. "Let the gestures of the body be agreeable to the matter of thy discourse. For it hath been ever held a solœsime in oratory, to poynt to the Earth, when thou talkest of Heaven."

Original French. "Parmy les discours regardez à mettre vostre corps en belle posture."

Were there space here for all the maxims they should be given, so quaint are they in phrase, so sound in foundation, resting upon the deep moral principle of consideration for others, and many of them applicable without change to modern requirements. But fragments of them must suffice :—

"Be not immodest in urging your Friends to discover a secret."

"Wear not your Cloths foul, unript, or dusty."

"Sleep not when others Speak, Sit not when others stand, Speak not when you should hold your Peace, walk not when others Stop."

"Superfluous Complements and all Affectation of Ceremony are to be avoided, yet where due they are not to be Neglected."

"Read no Letters, Books, or Papers in Company but when there is a Necessity for the doing of it you must ask leave: come not near the Books or Writ-

ings of Another so as to read them unless desired
. . . look not nigh when another is writing a
Letter.''

"Speak not of doleful things in a time of mirth.''

"Talk not with meat in your mouth.''

"Labour to keep alive in your breast that little
Spark of Celestial fire called Conscience.''

Such were the precepts that Washington copied
as a boy of fourteen, and they entered like leaven
into that young lump of strength. "Your future
character and reputation [he writes, forty-three
years afterward to a nephew] will depend very
much, if not entirely, upon the habits and manners
which you contract in the present period of your
life.'' These words are not the facile commonplaces
of an elderly man moralizing to a youth; they indicate that Washington was entirely aware of the
great influence for good exerted upon his own
character by the Rules of Civility. It is a misfortune for all American boys in all our schools to-day,
that they should be told the untrue and foolish story
of the hatchet and cherry tree, and denied the immense benefit of instruction from George Washington's authentic copy-book.

Ornamental knowledge he had no opportunity for
(with life's necessities pressing him so near), and
very likely he showed small leaning to it. It is plain
that his business bent was already strong in him,

and that beyond the necessity, his own instinct
chose the line of bonds and receipts, rather than of
literature and history. And yet they have been quite
wrong who at various times have asserted that he
was an ignorant man of but small reading. That he
read for practical purposes more than for entertainment is undoubtedly true, and that he held a very
humble opinion of his own taste and judgment in
literary matters is equally so—yet how interesting
is this passage in a letter written to Lafayette in
1788!—

"... Such are your Antient Bards who are both
the priest and door-keepers to the temple of fame.
And these, my dear Marquis, are no vulgar func-
tions ... heroes have made poets, and poets heroes.
Alexander the Great is said to have been enraptured
with the Poems of Homer. ... Julius Cæsar is well
known to have been a man of highly cultivated
understanding and taste. ... The Augustan Age
is proverbial ... in it the harvest of laurels and
bays was wonderfully mingled together. ... The
age of your Louis the fourteenth, which produced
a multitude of great poets and great Captains, will
never be forgotten; nor will that of Queen Ann ...
for the same cause. ... Perhaps we shall be found
at this moment, not inferior to the rest of the world
in the performances of our poets and painters; not-
withstanding many of the incitements are wanting

which operate powerfully among older nations. For it is generally understood, that excellence in those sister Arts has been the result of easy circumstances, public encouragements and an advanced stage of society. . . . I hardly know how it is that I am drawn thus far in observations on a subject so foreign from those in which we are mostly engaged, farming and politics. . . .''

It is not an ignorant man who writes thus. Somehow at some time during his life so full of sword and of plough, he had considered the poets and heroes, and the question of subsidized art, although the scanty glimpses that he gives of this consideration make us, who would know him wholly, regret that he was not more often ''drawn thus far in observations on a subject so foreign.''

At the age of fourteen—the age of the copy-book —he had a wish to enter the navy, which his mother opposed, and he therefore went on with his school and his mathematics, which led him to the study of surveying—a very important fact in his destiny. It was probably now, after his disappointment about the navy, that his home responsibilities grew clear to his conscience and that he absented himself from the playground for the sake of harder study. The girls used to wish that he would talk more; ''he was a very bashful young man,'' is the recorded opinion of one of them in later life; yet some girl had already disturbed his dawning passion. Presently he was writing verses, though of a quality scarce equal to his mathematics.

> "Oh ye Gods why should my Poor resistless Heart
>    Stand to oppose thy might and power —

*      *      *      *      *

> "In deluding sleepings let my eyelids close
>    That in an enraptured dream I may
> In a rapt lulling sleep and gentle repose
>    Possess those joys denied by day."

Other lyrics to other ladies are found in his early writing, but maturer passion ended by expressing itself in prose.

Such was the boy: of vigorous flesh, of grave spirit rendered graver by necessity, a respected umpire of school-ground disputes, a romantic follower of the fair sex; his hair was brown, his eye blue gray, not flashing but steady, and he had a nose that his friends must have hoped he would grow up to.

### III

So his schooldays ended, and with them not indeed his education, for this was just begun; but schoolmasters and copy-books were over, and the apronstring was broken. It was not beneath his mother's roof any more, but at Mount Vernon, with his

brother Lawrence, that his home was to be. Here
he was to turn his studies in surveying to practical
account, and to practical account also the rules of
civility. The working of these in his character and
demeanour brought him that next experience, that
next education, which may be set among the chief advantages of his youth. It would seem that the Mount
Vernon neighborhood was poor in gentlefolk compared to Fredericksburg, and that the manners and
breeding of this young Washington, who had come
here to live, shone out, and won for him at once the
notice of an older man of high position and noble
nature. Lord Fairfax lived on his estate adjoining
Mount Vernon. Belvoir, his place (pronounced
Beaver), could be seen from there across Dogue
Run, the little tributary of the Potomac so often
mentioned by Washington in his diaries. The boy
surveyor—he was not yet quite sixteen—spent his
steady working hours in going about over his
brother Lawrence's lands, running lines with admirable pains and accuracy, and his holidays he
took in hunting the fox. That he relaxed himself
between-whiles sometimes in the composition of
verse, full of the sighs of unrequited love, is less
remarkable at sixteen than the quality of his surveyor work. He fell in with Lord Fairfax while
surveying as well as while hunting, and the nobleman admired the energy which the lad put into both

work and play—but it may very well be that what
endeared the young surveyor to his lordship was
the gallant manner in which he took his fences.
"Let your recreations be Manfull not Sinfull," says
Rule 109 in the copy-book. And so Washington's
pluck, and his good, modest manners, brought Fairfax to make him his frequent companion in hunting
and his guest at Belvoir, where there were well-bred
women, and Addison's essays, and all was of a piece
of the same sound mellow civilization. In this good
society the boy of sixteen grew steadily into a man
of the world (though of his bashfulness he never became complete master, and we shall see this later
upon several occasions), and he also learned in
farming and agriculture those standards of English
thoroughness which he endeavored to maintain later
in the midst of the American slackness that prevailed then, as it prevails to-day. What he learned
among the ladies who lived or visited at Belvoir
came as naturally to him and was retained as tenaciously by his instinct and his memory as the outdoor knowledge, the planting, harvesting, fencing,
gates, hinges, and all else with which Lord Fairfax's
talk must have abounded, while the older man and
the young rode leisurely across country together
after a hunt. Fairfax was bound to comment upon
the slovenly American farming that they passed
by at such times.

Surely his lordship gave the boy a mount now
and then! Surely he sometimes said: "There's a
young horse at Belvoir you had better try and see
if he will do for the ladies." It is agreeable to
think of those huntings; of the hounds scudding
over Virginia's pleasant hills, and hard behind them
the ruddy-faced nobleman, with George not quite
abreast of him (Rule 57: "In walking . . . with
. . . a man of Great quality, walk not with him
cheek by jowl, but somewhat behind him")—George
therefore keeping himself a respectful second, con-
trolling the sinful desires of the spirit to be first—
and some love verses forgotten in his pocket. Then
in the field corners, by the edges of the covers,
stopping to bite a sandwich, surely his lordship
would bid the boy come up for a pull at his own
flask, and surely the boy, after a proper hesitation,
would take the pull! (Rule 40: "Strive not with
your superiors in argument.") And so the two ride
home, talking together after the hunt; perhaps the
boy stops to sup at Belvoir with Lord Fairfax, or
perhaps the hunt has taken them to the other side
of the country, and Lord Fairfax sups and sleeps
at Mount Vernon; and as he and his host, Lawrence
Washington, light their bedroom candles, and part
for the night, his lordship says:—

"Your brother's a fine lad, Mr. Washington. We
must do something for him, Sir."

And the eyes of the elder brother fill with tenderness and pride at the remark of Lord Fairfax, for
he knows it to be true. In the character of the boy
he had brought from Fredericksburg, to give a start
in life if he could, he had soon discerned a jewel of
great price, and his hopes and his love were set
upon him.

Next, Lord Fairfax "does something" for young
George, makes him surveyor of his great back lands,
and the happy boy of sixteen gets on his horse and
rides forth to his career. The day is marked in his
diary. "Fryday March 11th, 1747-8 Began my
Journey in company with George Fairfax, Esqr.;
we travell'd this day 40 miles to Mr. George Newels
in Prince William County."

That he knew these days for happy ones is not
likely, for his nature was not the sort that sits esti-
mating the present moment in reflection, but rather
fills it with action; yet in his writings the joy of the
new adventure is plain.

"Dear Richard . . . Since you received my letter in October last, I have not sleep'd above three
nights or four in a bed, but, after walking a good
deal all the day, I lay down before the fire upon a
little hay, straw, fodder or bearskin . . . with man,
wife and children, like a parcel of dogs and cats;
and happy is he who gets the berth nearest the fire."

Only the man that in his youth has known camp-

ing, and the joy that comes to him who in many
months of the wilderness has not "sleep'd above
three nights or four in a bed," can comprehend the
delight of life which the young Washington knew
at this time. When in afteryears he saw these Fairfax days—the backwoods surveyings and the home-
comings to his friend's house—saw this in the far
horizon of the past, across the great anxieties, disas-
ters, and triumphs that lay between himself and his
youth, it is thus that we find him writing:—

". . . None of which events, however, nor all of
them together, have been able to eradicate from my
mind the recollection of those happy moments, the
happiest in my life, which I have enjoyed in your
company . . . and it is matter of sore regret, when
I cast my eyes towards Belvoir, which I often do, to
reflect, the former inhabitants of it, with whom we
lived in such harmony and friendship, no longer re-
side there, and that the ruins can only be viewed as
the memento of former pleasures."

These touching and revealing words were written
from Mount Vernon, May 16, 1798, after he had
been twice President, to Mrs. Sarah Fairfax in England, where she had gone to live. She was the widow
of that George Fairfax with whom he began his surveying journey on that "Fryday" the 11th of
March, fifty years before.

He had forgotten the sorrows of that earlier time,

of which the following letter will give us a smiling glimpse:—

"Dear Friend Robin . . . My place of residence is at present at his Lordship's, where I might, was my heart disengaged, pass my time very pleasantly as there's a very agreeable young lady lives in the same house. . . . But as that's only adding fuel to fire, it makes me the more uneasy, for by often and inevitably, being in company with her revives my former passion for your Lowland beauty; whereas, was I to live more retired from young women, I might in some measure eliviate my sorrows, by burying the chaste and troublesome passion in the grave of oblivion. . . ."

Buried it was not, at once; on the contrary, the lover orders, with as many careful and exact details as if it were a survey, a highly fashionable coat to be made for him: ". . . on each side six buttonholes . . . the waist from the armpit to the fold to be exactly as long or longer than from thence to the bottom. . . ." This is only a part, less than a third, of his directions about this coat, and does it not read remarkably like a survey?

But coat and all, he did not win his Lowland beauty (whoever she was, for later guesses fit the facts imperfectly), and it is plain that he followed now the most usual and most wholesome course of youth—cured one love-wound by receiving another.

The next lady refused him twice, we know, how many more times we do not know; but when this case proved hopeless, too, young George again had recourse to the like-cures-like treatment, and not for the last time. With him it would seem to have proved invariably successful.

Why was he so unlucky in these affairs? Why did he so fail to win young women's hearts? He was strong, athletic, tall, a daring rider, his manliness had won the hearts of his brother and Lord Fairfax. What, then, was the matter? It is hard to come at the reason, and very likely there is no one reason. In his favour he had those personal attributes just enumerated, and beyond these, the public mark he was already beginning to make. Appointed public surveyor very soon, at the instance of Lord Fairfax, before he was twenty he had the position of adjutant-general with the rank of Major. These are bright trophies to flourish in the eyes of the fair. But we may be sure that he did not flourish them, that the modesty and respectfulness which so commended him to his elderly patron still always became bashfulness when with a young woman; it is moreover possible that his gravity, his lack of quick, light talk, frightened them off when it came to tying themselves to it for life. And last, but least by no means, let us remember his nose. It was a formidable feature—it never ceased to be so—and in these budding days of manhood, it beaked out of that young face in overweening scale. Corresponding to this nose without, was a character within, huge, forcible, out of scale with the immature years and experience of its possessor. Perhaps the reader has at some time known a friend or acquaintance who was more symmetrical at thirty than at twenty, who was slow in growing up to himself. Not a few men are so, and when a creature of Washington's moral dimensions comes upon earth, his early personality is sure to be somewhat ungainly. Moreover, he is certain to crowd those who are near him without meaning it, or even knowing it. With the best of intentions, with the most real modesty, Washington must have been not seldom an uncomfortable, unwieldy companion among those of his own age. If we think these things over, we feel that we may understand why the girls would not have him.

His minute directions about a coat have been seen above, and this care as to dress never left him. A proper appearance was one of the many things to which his mind, in due proportion, attended, and almost always with that same precision of detail which he gave to all the multitudinous matters, public and private, that he took up. So it was with the harness for his horses, and his carriage; we can find numerous directions written to England about

his wife's clothes! If the Lowland beauty and her
several successors had ever the faintest inkling that
their suitor would supervise their petticoats and
farthingales, we need speculate no further why they
one and all dismissed him. In the general panorama
of orders about apparel that mingles with his writings, the most interesting trait of all is the appro-
priateness; as he grows older, he orders more sober
garments. At no period, young or old, is it common
to find him as unspecific as this:—

"FORT CUMBERLAND, 14 May, 1755.
"DEAR BROTHER:
"As wearing boots is quite the mode, and mine
are in a declining state, I must beg the favor of you
to procure me a pair that is good and neat."

There is one more word to say about the surveys
of this frequent young lover; they suffered no
neglect through the preoccupations of his heart. So
accurate they were, that to this day they stand
unquestioned, wherever found.

What did they for his character?—Sleeping (as
he records) in "one thread bear blanket with
double its weight of vermin," or lodging "where we
had a good dinner . . . wine and Rum punch in
plenty, a good Feather Bed with clean sheets," or
having "our tent carried quite off with ye wind,"

or meeting Indians coming from war, who entertain him with a war-dance, jumping "about ye Ring in a most comicle manner." It was the apprenticeship, the seasoning; he was learning the alphabet of Trenton and Valley Forge, personal discomfort was nothing to his body or his mind that loved a pretty coat on the proper occasion. His rides, his camps, his river swimming and rough wandering brought him close to those who were to be his soldiers hereafter, and brought them close to him; he and Virginia learned to know each other. He became a woodsman, a pathfinder, a shrewd judge of wild country and of wild human nature, he wore an Indian hunting shirt—but remained civilized all the while. For Lord Fairfax was always there to come home to from the log-cabins; Lord Fairfax at Belvoir, or at Greenway Court his new place, and Lawrence Washington at Mount Vernon, and their visitors, of good manners and urbane knowledge of the great world—gentlemen and ladies—a society to hold the backwoods surveyor to his standards; and there were the books also, *The Spectator*, and other sound volumes that he evidently read beneath their roofs. Thus, while the wilderness entered into his strong body, many wholesome things entered into his strong brain, and tenaciously stayed there.

To us, because we never saw him, it is wonderful to find him adjutant-general of his district at

twenty; that is the age when our present privileged
youth is carrying brokers' messages, or stealing
signs at college. It was not wonderful to those who
did see him—his appointment was made easily.
After this, it is less wonderful (since we begin to
perceive how large his figure was growing in the
community) to find him at twenty-two chosen by
the Governor of Virginia to go to the agitated frontier upon a general mission of pacification among
the French, the Indians, and the restless colonists.
His dear brother Lawrence was now dead, whose
health for some years had been failing. A journey
to the Barbadoes had not brought Lawrence the
strength he had sailed there to seek, while to George
who accompanied him (the only occasion when
Washington was ever absent from our continent)
it had brought smallpox, of which his face carried
the marks all his life. But young Washington had
passed beyond the need of any protector. He returned from his mission to the Ohio—Venango,
Duquesne, let them here be named—having come
safe through many pitfalls of Indian treachery,
French diplomacy, and frozen rivers.

"There was no way [he writes] for getting over
but on a Raft; which we set about with but one
poor hatchet. . . . Before we were half way over
we were jammed in the Ice . . . the Rapidity of
the Stream . . . jerked me out into ten feet of

Water." Does this not seem like the wintry wraith of Trenton, prophetically rising?

"Our horses were now so weak . . . and the Baggage so heavy . . . myself and others . . . gave up our Horses for Packs . . . I put myself in an Indian walking dress, and continued with them three Days."

"Queen Aliquippa . . . expressed great concern that we had passed her. . . . I made her a present of a Watchcoat and a Bottle of Rum; which latter was thought much the best present of the Two."

These few lines are from many pages recording that journey; pages of hardihood, caution, and resource, with now and then a slight suggestion of amusement, like Queen Aliquippa and the rum.

Thus Major Washington came out from the backwoods, and into the backwoods was sent again almost at once, but now as Lieutenant-colonel Washington. All Virginia knew now that she had found a man. They wished him to head the troops raised to protect the king's land, but he wrote: "The command of the whole force . . . is a charge too great for my youth and inexperience." "Dear George," was the reply, "I enclose you your commission. God prosper you with it." So he was made second in command, but through the death of his superior officer became first before the campaign was over.

God did prosper him—though not in ways immediately visible—for the alphabet of preparation went on,—the severe alphabet of responsibility, injustice, privation, defeat. These, with hard recruiting, scarce horses, scarce men, and stingy pay, were his next apprenticeship. Washington, a colony Colonel, was paid less than a king's captain, and was moreover looked down upon by the king's captain; it was his first taste of that dull superciliousness in the mother country toward her own flesh and blood across the sea, which ended in the estrangement and loss of that flesh and blood for ever.

"I have not offered," Washington writes Governor Dinwiddie, "to control Captain Mackay in anything . . . but, sir, two commanders are . . . incompatible. . . . He thinks you have not a power to give commissions that will command him . . . that it is not in his power to oblige his men to work upon the road . . . whilst our faithful soldiers are laboriously employed. . . . I am much grieved to find our stores so slow advancing. God knows when we shall be able to do anything for to deserve better of our country."

There we have it vivid after a hundred and fifty years—the English officer nasty to his American superior officer, and the English enlisted man nasty to his fellow-American enlisted man, lounging by and letting him do the dirty, digging work! We

need to-day no longer take the stilted, absurd view
taught us in our schoolbooks, that England was a
"tyrant" and a "despot" to us; the facts will not
bear it. Every American every day is suffering ten
times the tyranny from trusts and labor-unions that
we suffered from England before the Revolution;
but between those lines of Washington's letter to
Dinwiddie, we catch a flash of that intolerable atti-
tude of the Englishman to the American then,
whose exasperating effect really did more to throw
the tea into Boston harbor and to write the Declaration of Independence than all the acts of Parliament put together. But how bright does the young
Washington shine out in that last burst of fervour,
where the little homely turn of grammar seems
somehow only to make him the more engaging!
"God knows when we shall be able to do anything
for to deserve better of our country."

Yes; the alphabet of preparation was going on,
was even forming into words; though as compared
with Trenton and Valley Forge, those future days
when the weight and the fate of a nation were to
hang like a millstone about his neck, such words
seem of but one syllable. He tasted defeat in this
Great Meadows campaign, and perfidy of colleagues, and the ingratitude of Dinwiddie—severe
but wholesome flavours for the future loser of Long
Island and Brandywine, the future comrade of

Gates, Conway, and Charles Lee. Good reason had
he likewise to lament his total ignorance of French,
since trusting to interpreters led to a number of
crooked results, by which his reputation was
clouded for a while. So once again he marched
back from Venango and Duquesne with his new
harvest of experience, meagre supplies, scarce
horses, faithless allies, his conduct questioned—and
in the end no victory. Yet, when all was sifted
clear, he came out of it so honorable and efficient
amid the general mismanagement, that the Legislature voted him public thanks. His ups and downs
in favour also resemble the days to come, when Congress at one moment was for superseding him, and
at the next made him military dictator. He got
at this time, too, an Indian name, as later, by the
British, he came to be known as "the Old Fox";—
but by that time he no longer spoke of any place
as "a charming field for an encounter," as he spoke
of Great Meadows in his unwhetted enthusiasm. It
was now that his young blood took joy in the sound
of bullets, and that he wrote of his strength: "I
have a constitution hardy enough to encounter and
undergo the most severe trials." We may be quite
sure that enormous enjoyment was constantly his,
and that peril and the meeting it salted his many
troubles; and also we may suspect it was the mental
trials of having his conduct questioned, more than

any bodily hardships, that caused the "loss of
health" he soon speaks of,—nor was the "loss" a
heavy one. It looks as if young Colonel Washington
had that impatience of any ailment, so common to
men who are almost invariably well, and that he
took his present indisposition with undue gravity.

Of English superciliousness and insolence he began to have repeated experiences, the king's officers
being the offenders; and it is no surprise to find
him thoroughly roused by the mean offer of a non-
descript sort of rank, a compromise, carrying no
pay—this in the face of the recent vote of thanks
for his services in the Great Meadows campaign,
where the responsibilities of chief in command had
devolved upon him. In answer to such an affront,
he writes: "If you think me capable of holding a
commission that has neither rank nor emolument
annexed to it, you must entertain a very contemptible opinion of my weakness, and believe me to be
more empty than the commission itself." So he goes
indignant to Mount Vernon (now become his own),
but it is not for long. Again, in spite of his mother,
he is off to the French and Indian wars, wishing
"earnestly to attain some knowledge in the military profession . . . under a gentleman of General
Braddock's abilities and experience."

Thus he marches to another encounter with ad-
versity—the worst yet. Again it is the old back-

woods trail, again Great Meadows, and again Venango and Duquesne, whose sounding names seem
to ring like bells of omen through the time of Washington's apprenticeship. This expedition repeated,
in greater dimensions, the trials and lessons of its
predecessor; British insolence, British stupidity,
with failure and catastrophe as the upshot. Braddock applied to the backwoods, against Indians, just
the same methods of warfare he had known in
settled communities with travelled roads, against
white men, and he by no means thanked Washington for offering suggestions about the habits
of Indians, and the trackless character of the
country.

It has often been said, and is said still, that Washington had no humour; but this has been pushed too
far—to the point, indeed, of attributing to him an
eternal gravity of appearance and a stiffness of
spirit that never stooped so low as fun. Let us
provide him with no trait he does not himself dis-
close, but neither let us rob him of any. Early in
this lamentable Braddock expedition, he writes of
an escort of eight men he had with him: "Which
eight men were two days assembling, but I believe
would not have been as many seconds dispersing if
I had been attacked." And about this same time:
"I have at last discovered . . . why Mrs. Ward-
rope is a greater favorite of Genl. Braddock than

Mrs. F—. . . . Nothing less, I assure you than a present of delicious cake and potted Woodcocks!'' Washington had a sense of fun, could be on occasion sedately jocular, and also (as shall be seen) could be surprised into outbursts of hilarity as violent as his occasional outbursts of rage. His undoubtedly restricted sense of humour was of its day, eighteenth century; and a retort of Goldsmith's to Dr. Johnson, while they were discussing the doctor's ability to write a fable about little fish, might fit the Father of our Country well: ''Why, Doctor, you could never write a fable about little fish, you would make them talk like whales!''

Upon this expedition Washington added to his experience of military blundering, civil incompetence, political jealousy, and starving commissariat, a very valuable new piece of knowledge— that British soldiers could run away. He says: ''The dastardly behavior of the Regular troops (so called) exposed those who were inclined to do their duty to almost certain death. . . . I tremble at the consequence this defeat may have upon our back settlers.'' But before the end, before his own miserable catastrophe and death, poor British Braddock dropped his superciliousness, and learned to respect his young Virginia aide. Washington has left words about him both friendly and just.

Once more he was at Mount Vernon, but busy, scraping troops together, after four bullets through

his coat and two horses shot under him, with such
a record of bravery shining through the clouds of
Braddock's misfortune, that a clergyman, in a ser-
mon, preached in Virginia and printed in Philadelphia and London, says: "That heroic youth,
Colonel Washington, whom I can not but hope
Providence has hitherto preserved in so signal a
manner for some important service to his country."
How strange seems the petulant complaint of John
Adams in after days, that Washington owed his
distinction to having married a rich wife! He was
now appointed commander-in-chief of all forces in
the colony, with 300 pounds compensation for his
personal losses and his conduct in the Braddock
campaign. His familiar letters at this time speak
of severe illness, impaired constitution, and damaged private fortune. "I have been upon the losing
order . . . for near two years," he gloomily remarks. But there is evidence, in a letter written to
him from the Fairfax house, of some alleviations:—

"DEAR SIR: After thanking Heaven for your safe
return I must accuse you of great unkindness in
refusing us the pleasure of seeing you this night.
. . . If you will not come to us to-morrow morning
very early we shall be at Mount Vernon.

"Sallie Fairfax.
"Ann Spearing
"Eliz'th. Dent."

Here was another sort of harvest from the French and Indian wars: four bullets through his coat, and two horses shot under him, atoned for bashfulness somewhat—perhaps had somewhat cured bashfulness, and so changed his aspect to the female eye, that if they could quite marry him, they almost would.

Alleviations did not prevent him from promptly starting reform in the militia laws to insure more strict instruction; the French and Indian War still framed the colonies in from North to South with a band of fire and death, and presently the young commander of Virginia's forces is riding forth upon a military mission to Boston, with many alleviations by the way, as his list of expenses discloses: "For treating ladies to Microcosm 1.8; loss at cards 8.; for a Hatt . . . for silver lace . . . for 2 pr. of Gloves . . . for Cockades . . . for Breeches buckle" etc.,—here are the relaxations of the stately but convivial young dandy, as he passes through Philadelphia and New York on his journey. There are no bullet-holes in those coats; but an arrow from Cupid seems again to have made a rent in one of them while he was in New York.

It was, however, still a young bachelor who went from these agreeable distractions back into the bloody Indian wars, where his manly heart was soon moved to its depths by pity. He writes Dinwiddie:

"I am too little acquainted, Sir, with pathetic language, to attempt a description of the people's distresses . . . but . . . I would be a willing offering to savage fury, and die by inches to save a people." He continued to taste the superciliousness of "Regular" toward "Provincial" officers (England's dense arrogance was laying up for her a cumulative retribution in the colonial heart), and for the first time he came in for the public servant's inevitable portion of newspaper abuse. This mongrel, heel-snapping breed of injustice nearly cost the colony his services; he declared that nothing but the danger of the times prevented his instant resignation. While recruiting, he had been perforce summary both as to men and horses, and the drunkenness of his soldiers at Winchester had driven him to speak excellent but incautious words of "Tippling Housekeepers." This brought a violent unpopularity down upon him; it is at this day most comical to read that they threatened to blow out his brains! Many incidents at this time show that high temper of his to have been shrewdly tried, and to have flashed out now and then,—as, for instance, in these angry sentences:—

"Your favor . . . came to hand. . . . In answer to that part, which relates to Colonel Corbin's gross and infamous reflection on my conduct last Spring, it will be needless, I dare say, to observe further at

this time, than that the liberty, which he has been
pleased to allow himself in sporting with my character, is little else than a comic entertainment, discovering at once . . . his inviolable love of truth,
his unfathomable knowledge, and the masterly
strokes of his wisdom in displaying it.''

At this time tired with campaigning, he was
evidently made ill by worry over Governor Dinwiddie's treacherous hostility toward him; he was
obliged to leave his post and go to Mount Vernon
to recover his strength. But political treachery and
hostility were again excellent things to become in-
ured to, else later, when our country's life depended
on him alone, they might have proved too much for
his unschooled endurance; nor should there go un-
mentioned, among the various branches of his education during these years of apprenticeship, a control of temper that would have been less perfect
had it been more complete; there are times when it
is best a man should let loose his rage.

It was nearly six months before his health allowed
him to resume his duties at Richmond, at which
time we find another lady in the case, and she seems
to have listened to him more seriously than did her
several predecessors. Was it fame? or had he
learned the art better? or was it that an ill-used,
invalid young Washington was more than the
female heart could withstand? No written docu-

ments guide us among these surmises. Besides love-
making, he was busy again with soldiers, and had
a troop dressed in Indian hunting garb, remarking
that "convenience rather than show . . . should be
consulted." In the Revolution, he recommended
this dress again, for the sake of its lightness and
general practicability, with some characteristic
words on the value of form in military dress, but
the greater importance of utility.

At last Fort Duquesne fell (it became Fort Pitt,
and then Pittsburgh) and the long tale of helpless
citizens, ill-fed troops, and political incompetence
came to an end. The bitter it held for Washington
was surely surpassed by the sweet: esteem and
recognition from thousands everywhere, far beyond
Virginia's boundaries, crowned by that final, that
perfect, that unique tribute from the Speaker of
the House of Burgesses, upon his installation as a
member of that body. He had met one sweeping
defeat at the polls, when the "Tippling Housekeepers" had taken their revenge on him; but now
this had been reversed by an equally sweeping victory. It was in Williamsburg, in May, 1759, when
Washington was twenty-seven years old, and commander-in-chief of all Virginia; when his first war
was over, when Montcalm and Wolfe had fallen.
In the House of Burgesses, Mr. Robinson, the
speaker had greeted the young member with such

praise and welcome in Virginia's name, that Washington was overcome. He rose, attempted to reply, blushed, and speech failed him. "Sit down, Mr. Washington," said the speaker, "your modesty is equal to your valor, and that surpasses the power of any language that I possess."

The mind, full of all that has happened to us since that May morning when the young Father of his Country stood in the House of Burgesses at Williamsburg, cannot dwell upon the scene without the heart being affected; Speaker Robinson spoke true. Does history contain, anywhere, a wreath of words more beautiful, which time has only set more surely upon its wearer's head? We leave him standing among the Burgesses, tall with his six-foot-three, strong and straight from his campaigns, grown comely and commanding, slender but large-made, a beautiful serene width between his eyes, blushing and trembling because they had praised him to his face.

## IV

"Mount Vernon, 20 September, 1759.

". . . The Scale of Fortune in America is turned greatly in our favor, and success is become the boon Companion of your Fortunate Generals. . . . I am now, I believe, fixed at this seat with an agreeable Consort for Life. And hope to find more happiness

in retirement than I ever experienced amidst a wide
and bustling world."

The invalid had prevailed in his courting; he
had been married on the 6th of the preceding
January to Martha Custis, widow of David Parke
Custis, and daughter of John Dandridge. She
brought to him and Mount Vernon a considerable
fortune, and she made later a gracious and dignified figure as the President's wife. Few of her
words or acts are recorded, but her discretion has
come down to us. In the mind's eye of the Nation
she sits forever, serene and kindly in her white cap
and kerchief, our country's first hostess. The gentle
haze of legend beneficently keeps her, as she should
be, a living but quiet spirit, watching from the soft
twilight of her privacy the destinies of the Republic
she played her part in founding.

It is no great strain of metaphor to say that
Washington had now his first chance to sit down
since the days when he had pored over his school
copy-book; in very truth it made a sort of pause,
a breath-taking, between the backwoods and the
Revolution, and he loved it best of all. That phrase
about his hoping to find more happiness in retirement than in a wide and bustling world was not an
elegant moral sentiment written because it was
then the heyday of elegant moral sentiments in
epistolary prose. His letters certainly show this

prevailing fashion of the time, but far less than those of Jefferson, for example,—less than almost any one's,—their sentences generally bearing very directly on some point of vital public or private necessity. He loved Mount Vernon; to be there with his garden, and his crops, and his animals, was his deepest heart's desire, and we do not need his word for it. Were his writings not full of the conscious and unconscious delight in it, and yearning for it, his conduct would be enough; whenever he can, he is always going back there, and when public service prevents, sighs often escape him in familiar letters —letters that he signs "With affectionate regard, I am always yours" instead of "I am &c.," or "I am, dear Sir, your most obedient &c.," or any of those reticent formulas he more commonly uses. It would not be ill (in a more elaborate account of him) to present in gradation the various manners in which he would close a letter; they reveal much of him and of the situation, from the "I am &c.," up to the rare "Yours affectionately," passing on the way such occasions as when an unknown lady has sent him a poem, or when the political matter is very delicate, and the person a foreigner of distinction, when he will say: "It affords an occasion also of assuring you, that, with sentiments of the highest esteem and greatest respect, I have the honor to be, &c."

For a while it was now his lot to be generally
at Mount Vernon instead of hurrying somewhere on
a horse with ragged soldiers behind him; this domestic and pastoral pause of about six years makes
the longest parenthesis in the rush of his public
existence that he ever knew. Its quiet was the quiet
of deep growth in character. We have seen that
he entered it a large man; he came out of it a great
man, ready for what awaited him. The process is
to us invisible; he never set down his meditations,
and the hairbreadth steps of increase elude the eye
as Spring does in turning to Summer; but evidently
he pondered, reached conclusions, ripened much,
was but little aware of it, and set no value upon
it at all as a matter of any possible interest to
others. And certainly he would have resented in-
quiries of a personal sort as unwarrantable inva-
sions of his privacy. Once in later life, his silence
when some of the clergy endeavored to force him
to declare his religious views, very plainly told
them that he considered their attempt a piece of
impertinence. It is singular that he should have
been made out a devout churchman by some, and
an atheist by others, when his own acts and writings
perfectly indicate what he was. He gave up taking
the Communion in middle life; he attended church
regularly as President, and not at all so when living
at Mount Vernon; in dying, he said nothing about

religion. His nature was deeply reverent, and his letters so abound in evidences of this that choosing among them is hard:—

(1778) "The hand of Providence has been so conspicuous in all this, that he must be worse than an infidel that lacks faith, and more than wicked, that has not gratitude enough to acknowledge his obligations."

(1791) "The great Ruler of events will not permit the happiness of so many millions to be destroyed."

(1792) "But as the All-wise Disposer of events has hitherto watched over my steps, I trust, that, in the important one I may be soon called upon to take, he will mark the course so plainly as that I cannot mistake the way."

(1794) "At disappointments and losses which are the effects of providential acts, I never repine, because I am sure the alwise disposer of events knows better than we do, what is best for us, or what we deserve."

These sentences are intentionally not taken from public papers, or formal letters, where convention might be the reason for their existence, but from letters to friends where nothing of the sort was demanded; they are therefore spontaneous expressions, as is this final one, written at a time of great stress:

(1798) "While I, believing that man was not
designed by the all-wise Creator to live for himself
alone, prepare for the worst that can happen."
These words probably state Washington's creed as
nearly and fully as it could be expressed; certainly
his deeds square with them fully. Do we count
among our public men any who lived less for himself alone?

But in these six years of quiet that he now entered upon at Mount Vernon he was able to follow
his inclinations, his private taste, to live for himself while the calm between the end of the French
and Indian War and the beginning of the Revolution lasted. He must have enjoyed the absence of
some things quite as much as the presence of others
—he must, for instance, have basked in the cessation of public criticism. It would be a great blunder to think of him as a man without nerves; he
was exceedingly sensitive. This quality, perhaps,
does not seem to fit with what he was else: a man
of far larger frame than common—his measure
after death being six feet three and a half inches—
with life-long sporting and outdoor tastes, with a
brain that worked by slow firm steps to secure conclusions; a man of moderation in food and drink,
though a lover of conviviality, a natural leader,
with almost indestructible endurance of body, and
completely indestructible endurance of spirit. This

is a character we should imagine impervious to
carp and cavil, being made of such stern stuff; but
it will not do to trust imagination in these matters.
It was in their foolish attempt to make of Washington what they imagined he ought to be—edify-
ingly super-human—that his early biographers
missed making him alive. The man himself, as he
has written himself unwittingly down for ever in
his letters and diaries—chokeful of vigour, nobility,
kindness, public spirit, now breaking out in a fury
at some newspaper attack, and now indulging in
sedate fun (somewhat broad at times)—such a man
is far more edifying than any concocted figurehead
of monotonously calm superiority. It has already
been said that Washington's ill-health at the close
of the French and Indian wars was more owing to
mental strain over the bad treatment he received
at Governor Dinwiddie's hands than to physical
hardship, and that he entertained thoughts of resigning which were expelled only by his sense of
patriotic responsibility. When this was past, he
did resign. We have also seen his trembling and
stammering under the embarrassment of praise in
public, and we shall see later his explosion of rage
at a political cartoon shown him during a cabinet
meeting. During the Revolution, he had a tiff with
Hamilton, and Hamilton went off in a huff; almost
at once Washington sent a message of amend to his
fiery young subordinate. It was a plain case of im-

patience on the General's part, and is another instance of his nerves. Jefferson wrote that he was
the most sensitive man to criticism that he knew.
But better than other men's opinions as to this is
what he writes himself. On receiving in December
1795, from the General Assembly of Maryland, a
declaration of loyalty and reliance, he responded
to the governor:—

"At any time the expression of such a sentiment
would have been considered as highly honorable
and flattering. At the present, when the voice of
malignancy is so high-toned . . . it is peculiarly
grateful to my sensibility."

Still more freely does he unveil his heart to a
nearer friend in 1796, and this passage is worth a
dozen opinions:—

"Having from a variety of reasons (among which
a disinclination to be longer buffeted in the public
prints by a set of infamous scribblers) taken my
ultimate determination 'to seek the post of honor
in a private station,' I regret exceedingly I did not
publish my valedictory address the day after the
adjournment of Congress. . . . It might have prevented the remarks which, more than probable,
will follow a late annunciation—namely, that I de-
layed it long enough to see that the current was
turned against me, before I declared my intention
to decline."

We find him, then, at sixty-seven, shrinking from

the "infamous scribblers" just as he had done at
twenty-seven—sensitive all his life long, in spite of
honours won, and the seasoning of struggle and of
age. These are the things, these contrasts, these
seeming contradictions in character, that strike the
flash of life, and let us see across the long dark
distance the heart of Washington beating, and the
blood surging to his face. It is fabricated con-
sistency that kills naturalness.

Of his humour, if humour it may be called, some
instances have been already given. But if we gather
before us all the anecdotes of this humour that record has preserved, and consider them as a whole,
they show rather a robust sense of fun, a wholesome power to be amused (and sometimes uproariously amused), than any subtle gift and percep-
tion. That Elizabethan roughness in mirth which
surges through Shakespeare and which still delights
the gallery to-day, in the eighteenth century still
delighted the boxes as well, all classes of society
taking a pleasure in "horse play," which a certain
portion of our community has now outgrown in its
decadent ascent from vigour to refinement. Washington seldom said droll things, but enjoyed very
heartily the droll things of others. We have the
story of his laughter when a young horse proved
too much for a boastful rider; of his laughter at
something told by a famous army raconteur while

the two were crossing the Hudson together; of his
laughter at a joke made by a visitor which threw
the whole Mount Vernon family into mirth, which
a parrot at once imitated, when Washington exclaimed: "Ah, you are a funny fellow. See, even
that bird is laughing at you." We have also the
account of how he laughed at General Putnam
(whom he called Old Put, being fond of him) on
an occasion which shall be mentioned later. We
have other instances, all showing a power to enjoy
what the Shakesperean audience enjoyed in the way
of fun;—in short, Washington's laughter may be
likened to a big bell that needs a good strong hand
to make it sound, and then rings out far over the
open fields. The light, quick tinkle of our electric
age was not anything that he knew, and perhaps
no story about this side of his nature is more vivid
than one told in a footnote in the life of Jeremiah
Smith, twice Chief Justice of New Hampshire, and
a visitor at Mount Vernon in 1797.

"Judge Marshall and Judge Washington (the
General's nephew Bushrod) were on their way to
Mount Vernon, attended by a servant who had the
charge of a large portmanteau containing their
clothes. At their last stopping place there happened
to be a Scotch pedlar, with a pack of goods which
resembled their portmanteau. The roads were very
dusty, and a little before reaching the general's,

they, thinking it hardly respectful to present themselves as they were, stopped in a neighboring wood
to change their clothes. The colored man got down
his portmanteau, and just as they had prepared
themselves for the new garments, out flew some
fancy soap and various other articles belonging to
the pedlar, whose goods had been brought on instead
of their own. They were so struck by the consterna-
tion of their servant, and the ludicrousness of their
own position, being there naked, that they burst
into loud and repeated shouts of laughter. Washington, who happened to be out upon his grounds
near by, heard the noise, and came to see what
might be the occasion of it, when, finding his
friends in that strange plight, he was so overcome
with laughter, that he actually rolled upon the
ground.''

Here, then, is an aspect of the Father of his
Country that has been sedulously kept from all the
generations of those whom the priggish, sickening,
cherry-tree invention has turned away from loving
him for being like themselves after all, and who
have given him, instead of their love, only a per-
functory, uninterested respect.

Judge Marshall saw him roll on the ground, but
Judge Marshall nevertheless told a friend within
three months of his own death that he was ''never
free from restraint in Washington's presence—

never felt quite at ease, such was Washington's
stateliness and dignity.''

Dignity and rolling on the ground are not incompatible; Washington's character is one of those rare
ones which not only can bear the whole truth, but
which gains by the whole truth. Another passage
from Jeremiah Smith's life will give, as well and as
simply as any of the contemporary memories, a
glimpse of Washington the man, the host in his own
house. The visitor arrived late in the afternoon—

''. . . And received a most cordial welcome from
Washington and his lady, the latter 'at this time
a squat figure, without any pretension to beauty,
but a good motherly sort of woman.' After a cup
of excellent tea &c., the evening passed in conversation. There were present, besides the family, a
son of Lafayette, and another French gentleman.
While they were talking, a servant came into the
room and said to Washington, 'John would like the
newspaper, sir.' He replied, 'You may take it,'
but after he had gone out, said, 'he had better
mind his work.' He then told Mr. Smith a story
of his coachman, a long-tried and faithful man.
One very rainy day he was obliged to order his
carriage unexpectedly, to go a long distance on
business. After getting into it he perceived that
there was some delay about starting, and putting
his head out, he saw that there was a great bustle

among his servants, who were trying to mount the
coachman on the box, and with much difficulty, at
length succeeded. 'What is the matter?' asked the
general. The servants replied, that he was intoxi-
cated; 'whereupon,' said Washington to Mr. Smith,
'I was tempted to say to the man at once, be gone
about your business.' But the coachman at that moment turned round and said, 'never fear, massa,
I'll drive you safe.' 'And I trusted him,' continued
Washington, 'and he never drove me better.'

"At about half past nine, Mr. Smith signified
his intention of retiring, when Washington also
arose, and taking a lamp, led the way to a most
comfortable apartment, in which was a fire brightly
blazing. He assured his guest that the fire 'would
be perfectly safe,' and intimated that he might
'like to keep his lamp burning through the night.'
In the morning, after breakfast, Mr. Smith took
leave, though desired to prolong his visit; and a
very urgent invitation was given, that he should
'bring his bride to see them.' Horses were brought
to the door, and Washington accompanied him some
miles on the way. 'He was always,' said Mr. Smith,
'dignified, and one stood a little in awe of him.' "

"A little in awe"; again that touch, given above
by Judge Marshall, and by so many others—in fact,
unanimously given. That Judge Marshall, himself
a considerable man, should have seen Washington

roll on the ground with laughter, yet after that
still never feel quite at ease in his presence is
wonderfully significant of the majestic figure that
Washington must have become after bearing our
young country on his shoulders through so many
years of its weakness and need. The truth is, a
great man cannot do great things without in a way
growing apart from his fellows, little as he may
desire such a result. For somewhat the same reason
the sight of a huge flood, or a deep chasm, or a
high mountain, inclines all save stunted spirits to
silence, and personal greatness distills inevitable
constraint, and draws around itself unknowingly
a circle of isolation that is not without its sadness.
In Washington's very last years, we read that during a dance of young people at Mount Vernon, he
came out of his study to take pleasure in looking
on, when a quiet spread over the gayety of the
party. It was explained that his presence caused
it, and then they saw that tall, weather-beaten figure go back to his solitude from the lights and the
laughter whose brightness he was unwilling to dim.

To the little glimpse of Mount Vernon privacy
given by Jeremiah Smith—the servant asking for
the newspaper, the tale of the coachman, the host
lighting his guest to the room with the brightly
burning fire—this further picture is worth select-
ing from the many that have survived. A visitor,

who was afflicted with a heavy cold, lay coughing
in his bed, unable to sleep, when he became aware
of the looming, night-clad form of Washington approaching his bed-side. Washington was bringing
him a bowl of tea which he had got out of his bed to
make himself for his guest's relief.

It is likely that Washington's familiar talk with
his friends (in those rare moments when they were
not all obliged to be debating the gravest possible
matters) was not infrequently relieved by touches
of that sedately expressed fun which occur now and
then in his letters, such as the passage about General Braddock and the potted woodcocks. Indeed,
we know that he could be jocular in the very heart
of a crisis. On that memorable night of Trenton,
in the midst of the icy, dangerous Delaware, he
turned to Henry Knox with a rough joke that still
lives upon the lips of men. But to men's lips it
must be confined; a printed page is not the place
for it, any more than a china-shop is the place for
a bull, who is an object as excellent in the fields
as Washington's speech was excellent on the Delaware, in the presence only of Knox and the boat-
man. His enjoyment of hunt-dinners, and of those
songs and jests which come after them, is well
known, and his fondness for theatrical shows, and
shows in general, was life-long, as was his pleasure
in dancing. He danced during war, as well as in

peace, and up to within three years of his death—
that is to say, when he was sixty-four years old.
Perhaps none of his letters better shows the changing from seriousness to amusement, and back
again, than the following to Lafayette:—

MOUNT VERNON, 10 May, 1786.

"MY DEAR MARQUIS,

". . . It is one of the evils of democratical gov-
ernments, that the people, not always seeing and
frequently misled, must often feel before they can
act right; but then evils of this nature seldom fail
to work their own cure. It is to be lamented,
nevertheless, that the remedies are so slow, and
that those who may wish to apply them seasonably
are not attended to before they suffer in person, in
interest, and in reputation. The discerning part of
the community have long seen the necessity of giving adequate powers to Congress for national purposes, and the ignorant and designing must yield
to it ere long. . . . The British still occupy our
posts to the westward. . . . It is indeed evident
to me that they had it in contemplation to do this
at the time of the treaty. The expression . . .
which respects the evacuation . . . is strongly
marked with deception. I have not the smallest
doubt, but that every secret engine is continually

at work to inflame the Indian mind, with a view to keep it at variance with these States for the purpose of retarding our settlements to the westward, and depriving us of the fur and peltry trade of that country.

"Your assurances, my dear Marquis, respecting the male and female asses, are highly pleasing to me, I shall look for them with much expectation. . . .

"The Jack which I have already received from Spain, in appearance is fine; but his late royal master, tho' past his grand climacteric, cannot be less moved by female allurements than he is; or when prompted can proceed with more deliberation and majestic solemnity to the work of procreation. . . .

". . . Your late purchase of an estate in the colony of Cayenne, with a view of emancipating the slaves on it, is a generous and noble proof of your humanity. Would to God a like spirit would diffuse itself generally into the minds of the people of this country. But I despair of seeing it. Some petitions were presented to the Assembly, at its last session, for the abolition of slavery, but they could scarcely obtain a reading. To set them afloat at once would, I really believe, be productive of much inconvenience and mischief; but by degrees it certainly might, and assuredly ought to be effected; and that too by legislative authority."

The jack received from Spain was named Royal
Gift in honor of the King's courtesy and compliment to Washington in waiving the law against
sending any of that particular breed out of the
country, and the animal was the occasion of several
other passages in Washington's letters, similar in
spirit to that in which he wrote Lafayette.

The breeding of animals was something to which
he much attended, he led all his neighbour planters
in discovering that there could be no profit in
tobacco, while in foreign ports any flour bearing
the brand "George Washington, Mount Vernon,"
was passed without further inspection, because his
honest goods had carried their reputation even over
the seas.

With his small book learning, his general leaning to sport and the open air, and his uncertain
spelling (even in the letter about his marriage, a
part of which begins this chapter, he speaks of
London as the great Matrapolis) we meet another
flash of contradiction in the discovery that he de-
cidedly liked to write. He plainly relished filling
pages with his sentiments and opinions, and that
beautiful manuscript of his must have been a quick
operation, which it certainly does not seem in appearance. Yet this, with his well-nigh miraculous
energy, is the only explanation of how a man, so
occupied in action as he was, managed to pen lit-
erally thousands of pages with his own hand. There

can be no doubt, when we turn over the fourteen volumes of his published writings, each of four hundred fifty pages, and by no means including the entire product of his pen (they omit seven hundred and one letters and addresses published elsewhere), that quite aside from letters of obligation, George Washington enjoyed sitting down to paper, quill, and ink, and that when he once got under way, he was quite likely to fill the sheet. Sitting down to other things was less apt to be so welcome,—sitting for his portrait, for instance, of which he writes:—

"At first I was . . . as restive under the operation, as a colt is of the saddle. The next time I submitted very reluctantly, but with less flouncing. Now, no drayhorse moves more readily to his thills than I to the painter's chair."

In this diverting account of his own progress toward resignation, we may read either his recognition that as a public man he must submit, or else that he came to enjoy it. However this may be, his sundry contacts with artists—painters, sculptors, and architects when it came to planning the Federal City (as it was called before his name was given to it)—led him to form an opinion of the "irritable race" which he expressed with the same happy unmistakableness that characterizes all his opinions:—

"It is much to be regretted, however common the case is, that men, who possess talents which fit them for peculiar purposes, should almost invariably be under the influence of an untoward disposition, or are sottish, idle, or possessed of some other disqualification, by which they plague all those with whom they are concerned. But I did not expect to have met with such perverseness in Major L'Enfant. . . ." And writing two years after this about another architect, his mind peeps forth again: "Some difficulty arises with respect to Mr. Hallet . . . his feelings should be saved and soothed as much as possible."

No one seems ever to have written letters more natural, more redolent of their writer, than Washington; those of many other eminent men—Jefferson, for example—often subtly betray a sense of being composed; but to read the correspondence of the master of Mount Vernon is gradually to feel one's self in his presence, almost as if the man were sitting there, and this quality is, if possible, more striking still in his domestic journal, from which we give a few foreshortened strokes, in order to paint Mount Vernon life in his own words, written during the early years of his marriage.

"Several of the family were taken with the measels. . . . Hauled the Sein and got some fish, but was near being disappointed of my Boat by means

of an oyster man who had lain at my Landing and
plagued me a good deal by his disorderly behavior. . . . Mrs. Washington was a good deal
better to-day but the oyster man still continuing
his Disorderly behavior at my landing, I was
obliged in the most preemptory manner to order
him and his company away. . . .

"Went to Alexandria and saw my Tobo . . . in
very bad order . . . visited my Plantation. Severely reprimanded young Stephens for his insolence. . . . After breakfast . . . rid out to my
Plantns . . . found Stephens hard at work with an
ax—very extraordinary this! . . . White Frost
. . . two negroes sick . . . ordered them to be
blooded . . . Stephens at Winchester. Visited my
Plantation and found to my great surprise Stephens
constantly at work . . . passing by my Carpenters
. . . I found . . . George, Tom, Mike and young
Billy, had only hugh'd 120 foot yesterday from 10
o'clock. Sat down therefore, and observed—

"Tom and Mike in a less space than 30 minutes,
cleared the bushes . . . visited my plantations before sunrise, and forbid Stephens keeping any
horses upon my expense." Stephens, by this time,
had probably learned to quake in his shoes. "Went
to a ball at Alexandria, where Musick and dancing
was the chief entertainment . . . great plenty of
bread and butter, some biscuits with tea and coffee,

which the drinkers of could not distinguish from
hot water sweetened . . . I shall therefore distinguish this ball by the stile and title of the Bread and
Butter Ball, . . .

"After several efforts to make a plow . . . was
feign to give it up. . . . Mrs. Posy and some young
woman, whose name was unknown to anybody in
this family, din'd here. . . . Spent the greatest
part of the day in making a new plow of my own
invention. . . . Sat my plow to work and found
she answered very well. . . . A messenger came to
inform me that my Mill was in great danger . . .
got there myself just time enough to give her a
reprieve . . . by wheeling dirt into the place which
the water had work'd."

He took off his coat in this emergency, and la-
bored with his men, and he probably did so on
many another occasion. Such a way of not merely
owning, but mastering, his property, brought him
to a most thorough and sagacious knowledge of the
soil. It were easy to overload our narrative with ex-
tracts from the copious pages of his agricultural
and domestic notes, and this must not be done; but
to omit these altogether would cause the reader to
miss a direct sight of Washington the farmer and
of his astounding power of detail.

"Harrowed the ground at Muddy Hole, which
had been twice ploughed, for Albany pease in

broad-cast. At Dogue Run began to sow the remainder of the Siberian wheat . . . ordered a piece
of ground, two acres, to be ploughed at the Ferry
. . . to be drilled with corn and potatoes between,
each ten feet apart, row from row of the same kind.
Sowed in the Neck . . . next to the eleven rows of
millet, thirty-five rows of the rib-grass seeds, three
feet apart and one foot asunder in the rows.'' (This
was the 14th of April, 1792.)

"*Corn.* On rows 10 feet one way, and 18 inches
thick single stalks; will yield as much to the Acre
in equal ground, as at 5 feet each way with two
stalks in a hill; to that Potatoes, Carrots, & Pease
between the drilled Corn, if not exhaustive, which
they are declared not to be, are nearly a clear
profit. . . . Let the hands at the Mansion House
grub *well,* and perfectly prepare the old clover
lot. . . . When I say grub *well,* I mean that everything, which is not to remain as trees, should be
taken up by the roots . . . for I seriously assure
you, that I had rather have *one acre* cleared in this
manner, than four in the common mode. . . . It is
a great and very disagreeable eye-sore to me, as
well as a real injury in the loss of labor and the
crop (ultimately), and the destruction of scythes,
to have foul meadows. . . .

"You will be particularly attentive to my negros
in their sickness; and to order every overseer *posi-*

*tively* to be so likewise; for I am sorry to observe that the generality of them view these poor creatures in scarcely any other light than they do a draught horse or ox . . . instead of comforting and nursing them when they lye on a sick bed. . . .

"Doll at the Ferry must be taught to knit, and *made* to do a sufficient day's work of it. . . . Lame Peter, if no body else will, must teach her. . . . Tell house Frank I expect he will lay up a more plenteous store of the black common walnut. . . .

"The deception with respect to the potatoes (210 instead of 418 bushels) is of a piece with other practices of a similar kind . . . for to be plain, Alexandria is such a recepticle for everything that can be filched from the right owners by either blacks or whites. . . . Workmen in most countries, I believe, are necessary plagues;—in this, where entreaties as well as money must be used to obtain their work, and keep them to their duty, they baffle all calculation. . . . If lambs of *any kind* have been sold . . . it has not only been done without my consent, but expressly contrary to my orders. And sure I am, the money for which they were sold never found its way into my pockets. . . . And I wish you would reprehend the overseers severely for suffering the sheep under their respective care to get so foul as I saw some when I was at home.

. . . It is impossible for a sheep to be in a thriving condition when he is carrying six or eight pounds at his tale.—And how a man who has them entrusted to his care, and must have a sight of this sort every day before his eyes can avoid being struck with the propriety and necessity of easing them of this load, is what I have often wondered at. . . .

"It is to be observed, by the weekly reports, that the sewers make only six shirts a week, and the last week Carolina (without being sick) made only five. Mrs. Washington says their usual task was to make nine with shoulder straps and good sewing. . . .

"Desire Thomas Green to date his reports. . . . I fancy it will puzzle him to make out 508 feet in the twenty four plank there set down. . . . How does your growing wheat look at this time? I hope no appearance of the Hessian fly is among it. . . . In clearing the wood, mark a road by an easy graduated ascent from the marsh . . . up the hollow which leads into the lot beyond the fallen chestnut . . . and leave the trees standing thick on both sides of it . . . if too thick, they can always be thinned; but, if too thin, there is no remedy but time to retrieve the error. . . .

"Spring Barley . . . has thriven no better with me than Vetches. . . . Of the field Peas of England I have more than once tried, but not with

encouragement to proceed. . . . The practice of
plowing in Buckwheat twice in a season, as a fer-
tilizer, is not new to me. . . . The cassia charmœ-
crista, or Eastern shore Bean . . . has obtained a
higher reputation than it deserves. . . . I am not
surprized that our mode of fencing should be disgusting to a European eye . . . no sort of fencing
is more expensive or wasteful of timber. . . .

"I find by the reports that Sam is, in a manner,
always returned sick; Doll at the Ferry, and several of the spinners very frequently so, for a week
at a stretch; and ditcher Charles often laid up with
a lameness. I never wish my people to work when
they are really sick . . . but if you do not examine
into their complaints, they will lay by when no
more ails them than all those who stick to their
business. . . . My people . . . will lay up a month,
at the end of which no visible change in their
countenance, nor the loss of an oz. of flesh is dis-
coverable; and their allowance of provision is going on as if nothing ailed them. . . . What sort of
lameness is Dick's . . . and what kind of sickness
is Betty Davis's . . . a more lazy, deceitful and im-
pudent huzzy is not to be found in the United
States. . . . I am as unwilling to have any person,
in my service, forced to work when they are unable, as I am to have them skulk from it, when
they are fit for it. . . . Davy's lost lambs carry

with them a very suspicious appearance. . . . If some of the nights in which . . . overseers are frolicking . . . were spent in watching the barns, visiting the negro quarters at unexpected hours, waylaying the roads, or contriving some device by which the receivers of stolen goods might be entrapped . . . it would redound much more to their own credit . . . than running about. . . . I . . . give it as a positive order, that after saying what dog or dogs shall remain, if any negro presumes under any pretence whatsoever to preserve, or bring one into the family, that he shall be severely punished and the dog hanged. I was obliged to adopt this practice whilst I resided at home . . . for the preservation of my sheep and hogs; but I observed when I was at home last, that a new set of dogs was rearing up, and I intended to have spoke about them. . . . It is not for any good purpose negros raise or keep dogs, but to aid them in their night robberies; for it is astonishing to see the command under which their dogs are. . . . The practice of running to stores &c. for everything that is wanting, or thought to be wanting . . . has proved the destruction of many a man. . . . I well know that things must be bought . . . but I know also that expedients may be hit upon and things (though perhaps not quite so handsome) done within ourselves, that would ease the expenses of my estate very considerably.''

These quotations, it will be understood, come
from no one passage, but are taken from many,
written at widely different dates, sometimes in the
form of notes, and sometimes addressed to those in
charge of Mount Vernon when its master was
obliged to be away attending to the Revolution,
or the Constitutional Convention, or the duties of
President. What is here given is perhaps a thous-
andth part of the whole, and as we discern Doll at
the Ferry and ditcher Charles, and the superfluous
dogs, sitting in the back paths and crossroads of
Washington's immortality, we see himself, in
neither military nor state dress, but easy in his
home riding clothes, passing over his fields at sunrise, watching the Siberian wheat, pointing where a
new road should go, where a new tree should rise,
and happier in those pastoral hours than his more
glorious moments ever beheld him. Upon this side
of his life and character we cannot dwell again, save
now and then to remind the reader that it lay always in the depths of his heart, no matter what else
that "spark of celestial fire called conscience"
might be driving him to do in the service of his
country; we finish our detailed reference to it, with
what he wrote Hamilton at the time he was considering his last speech to Congress.

"It must be obvious to every man, who considers
the agriculture of this country, (even in the best
improved parts of it) and compares the produce of

our lands with those of other countries, no ways
superior to them in *natural fertility,* how miserably
defective we are in the management of them; and
that if we do not fall on a better mode of treating
them, how ruinous it will prove to the landed interest. Ages will not produce a systematic change
without public attention and encouragement; but
a few years more of increased sterility will drive
the Inhabitants of the Atlantic states westwardly
for support; whereas if they were taught how to
improve the old, instead of going in pursuit of new
and productive soils, they would make those acres
which now scarcely yield them anything, turn out
beneficial to themselves—to the Mechanics by supplying them with the staff of life on much cheaper
terms—to the Merchants, by increasing their Commerce and exportation—and to the Community generally, by the influx of Wealth resulting therefrom.
In a word, it is in my estimation, a great national
object, and if stated as fully as the occasion and
circumstances will admit, I think it must appear
so.''

At his death in 1799, plans of crops were found
written out for 1800, 1801, 1802, and 1803.

His marriage brought him no children, save
those of other people—two step-children, and a suc-
cession of nephews, nieces, grand-nephews, and
grand-nieces, these latter littering his domestic life

with the responsibilities which their parents had failed to meet. Their support and rearing were loaded upon him, and strung out over a quarter of a century; some of them lived with him, and he was endlessly paying out money for the others—for their food, their clothes, their education, and sometimes for their debts, as he had likewise done on occasion for their incompetent fathers. "Dear Sir [he writes Samuel Washington, the son of his worthless brother Samuel] I perceive by your letter of the 7th Instant that you are under the same mistake that many others are—in supposing that I have money always at command. The case is so much the reverse . . . that I found it expedient to sell all my lands (near 5000 acres) in Pennsylvania . . . Be assured there is no practice more dangerous than that of borrowing money (instance as proof the case of your father and uncles) . . . all that I shall require is, that you will return the net-sum when in your power, without Interest." Many are the letters like this, beginning with a lecture and ending with a kindness—and many of the loans were still unpaid when he died; in his will some are expressly released. Nor was it his own blood alone; his wife's relations come in for his help, and her grandchildren. In one case we find, "Mrs. Haney should endeavor to do what she can for herself—this is a duty incumbent on every one; but you must not let her suffer, as she has thrown herself upon me.''—What relation Mrs. Haney was to him, nobody has been able to find! Though the whole of this miscellaneous brood of dependents did not turn out as worthless as some of them did, his unceasing generosity and watchful care may be said to have been really rewarded in the cases only of Bushrod Washington, his nephew, and Nelly Custis, his wife's grand-daughter. To her he was devoted, as his constant gifts, and his letters show, while of Bushrod he was both proud and fond. But he had a niece Harriot, whose name ends by bringing an expectant smile to the lips whenever one comes to a letter addressed to her or a reference made to her. In her way, she evidently annoyed her uncle as much as did Doll at the Ferry, or the oyster man, and when one finally meets a passage alluding to her conduct, which ''I hear with pleasure has given much satisfaction to my sister,'' the smile becomes laughter. When the various boys fallen upon his hands begin to go to school and to college, the good Washington's letters to them abound in affectionate wise counsel as to their work, their play, their dress, their company, their habits; twice, first to Bushrod and then to George Steptoe Washington (a grand-nephew) long afterward, he writes that he is no stoic to ask too much of young blood. Not the least touching point

in the many documents which record his relations
with all these young people is to find in his expense
accounts: "The Wayworn traveller, a song for
Miss Custis," and for his young step-children in
his early married life, "10 shillings worth of Toys,"
"6 little books for children beginning to read," "A
box of Gingerbread Toys & Sugar Images or
Comfits."

A passage at the close of one of his letters, written when he was above sixty (with Mrs. Washington in good health), gravely speculating upon
the possibility of his marrying again, is in keeping
with his habit of weighing all contingencies; one of
his brothers had five wives, he was Mrs. Washington's second husband, what if he survived her? He
renounces the hope of children, for, he says, he
would not commit the folly of taking a young wife,
but a partner suitable to his years. The whole
paragraph is a very natural one, if scarcely romantic, and we may be certain it would have been little
pleasing to Mrs. Washington. It should not be a
matter of regret to us, but rather one of relief,
that he was childless. The spectacle of a great
man's children and grandchildren is so seldom edifying, and so often mortifying, that on the whole it
is better none of his direct blood is among us, and
that he stands alone, with no weeds of posterity
clogging round his feet. There is but one family

in all America whose name forms an unbroken
chain of public service and honour, from its progenitor to the present day; in this country the
abolition of primogeniture makes such families
well-nigh impossible, and with the gain achieved by
such abolishment goes the loss of hereditary family
responsibility to the State,—a loss so far not balanced by the civic responsibility manifested by the
American citizen as a unit. The life and property
of the Englishman are to-day better protected than
the life and property of the American, and this is
owing, in the last analysis, to a better public opinion and better legislative efficiency in England.
Many a "younger son" has gone into politics and
parliament, and shone there, because of this sense
of hereditary family duty to the State. How many
of their American equivalents are in Congress and
the Senate?

It has been said—quite falsely—that Washington made his wife unhappy. A number of these
scandals have a clergyman for their source; but no
more than some lawyers can kill our ideal of Justice, are some parsons able to disgust us with Religion. The various tales have been tracked down
to the nothing they started from, even the apparently solid one of the Virginia tombstone bearing a
name and the words, "The natural son of Washington." There is no such tombstone, and never

was. Most of these forgeries originated during the time of the Conway Cabal, when Lee (of Monmouth dishonour), and Gates, and others put their hands to anything that might hurt Washington; but it was themselves that the pitch ultimately defiled. Through Washington's forty years of married life there was constant mutual devotion between his wife and himself, reliance upon him from her, and from him solicitude for her when the war kept them apart, and affection when they were together. While Mr. Lear, his last secretary, and Dr. Craik, his warm friend and physician, were at his death-bed, "fixed in silent grief, Mrs. Washington, who was sitting at the foot of the bed, asked with a firm and collected voice, 'Is he gone?'" Mr. Lear could not speak but held up his hand as a signal that he was. "'Tis well,' said she in a plain voice. 'All is now over. I have no more trials to pass through. I shall soon follow him.'" [This is from Lear's account.] And on the next day, "Mrs. Washington desired that a door might be made for the Vault, instead of having it closed up as formerly, after the body should be deposited, observing, 'That it will soon be necessary to open it again.' From that day, she moved from their room to a little room above it, which had the only window in the house whence his grave could be seen. There she lived until she followed him."

Into the quiet of Mount Vernon, some six years after Washington's marriage, broke the rumours and rumblings that were to end in Revolution, and from that time on his mind was increasingly aroused. We may perhaps set our finger upon the very day that saw him waken to resentment against England,—*home* as he called her to the last possible moment,—the 29th of May, 1765, when the House of Burgesses at Williamsburg was thrown into debate "most bloody" (as Jefferson describes it) by certain seven resolutions moved by an uncouth young rustic of genius. Patrick Henry had already severely disconcerted the established leaders of Virginia by his argument in the "Parsons' Cause" in December, 1763, when the wrong side, through him, had won. But on this occasion, by those resolutions about taxation offered by this new member, and by his speech—"if this be treason, make the most of it"—places were changed, and Peyton Randolph, Richard Bland, George Wythe, and Edmund Pendleton, sorely against their judgment and liking at first, followed the lead of Patrick Henry into the Revolution. We can see the progress of Washington's mind through the next ten years in brief fragments of his letters—those ten years that saw Franklin before Parliament, the Boston "massacre" (a large name to have given it), the tea tax (after which Washington went without all taxed

articles), the Burgesses' many dissensions with the
royal governors, the Boston Tea Party, the Boston
Port Bill, the Continental Congress to which he
rode as delegate with Pendleton and Henry, and
at length the outbreak of war:—

"The Stamp Act . . . engrosses . . . conversation . . . many luxuries . . . can well be dis-
pensed with . . . where, then, is the utility of
these restrictions? . . . Great Britain will be satisfied with nothing less than the deprivation of
American freedom. . . . Yet arms . . . should be
the last resource. . . . Is it against the duty of
three pence per pound on tea? . . . No, it is the
right only . . . Great Britain hath no more right
to put . . . hands into my pocket . . . than I have
to put hands into yours. . . . I could wish, I own,
that the dispute had been left to posterity. . . . If
it can not be arrested . . . more blood will be
spilled . . . than history has ever yet furnished instances of in North America. . . . I am well satisfied that no such thing is desired by any thinking
man in all North America . . . that it is the ardent wish . . . that peace . . . upon constitutional
grounds, may be restored. . . . I can solemnly declare to you, that, for a year or two past, there has
been scarce a moment that I could properly call my
own, that with my own business, my present ward's,
my mother's, Colonel Colville's, Mrs. Sawyer's,

Colonel Fairfax's, Colonel Monro's, and . . . my brother Augustine's concerns . . . together with the share I take in public affairs . . . I have really been deprived of every kind of enjoyment.''

At the time he rides to the Continental Congress, an account of him is given by a fellow Virginian among a number of pithy descriptions: Of Randolph, ''a venerable man . . . an honest man . . . a true Roman spirit''; of Bland, ''a wary, old, experienced veteran . . . has something of the look of old musty parchments, which he handleth and studieth much''; of Henry, ''in religious matters a saint; but the very devil in politics; a son of thunder''; and of Washington, ''a soldier,—a warrior; he is a modest man; sensible; speaks little; in action cool, like a bishop at his prayers.''

Yes, he spoke little, and his quiet, with so much wisdom behind his rare words, must have been a balm in that Babel of bickering and jealousy. The ''Fathers'' did not sit in an exalted harmony of patriotism and knee-breeches, as they have been too often pictured to us; it was with them a cat-and-dog affair, not seldom, as it is with us; this it is better to know plainly, to save us from that shallow error of lamenting that in every respect we have fallen away from them. At any one moment of the world, there are thousands of times more fools alive than wise men, but in spite of this, we

fall heirs to what the wise men accomplished, while
the fools' work is mostly perishable in the long run.

The journal of the Continental Congress discloses, in spite of its cautious meagreness, that the
Fathers were inharmonious. "Tuesday, Sep. 6,
1774 . . . *Resolved,* That in determining questions
in this Congress, each Colony or Province shall have
one Vote.—The Congress not being possess'd of
. . . materials for ascertaining the importance of
each Colony." "The difficulty to be met was raised
by Virginia, who claimed a prominence that the
delegates from other Colonies were unwilling to
concede." [Connecticut delegates to Governor
Trumbull, Oct. 10, 1774.] We have further, and
more piquant, elucidations from the diary of John
Adams, whose nerves were frequently jangled by
his colleagues. "Oct. 24, Monday. In Congress,
nibbling and quibbling as usual. There is no
greater mortification than to sit with half a dozen
wits deliberating upon a petition, address, or memorial. These great wits, these subtle critics, these
refined geniuses, these learned lawyers, these wise
statesmen, are so fond of showing their parts and
powers, as to make their consultations very tedi-
ous." Thus he frets, in wholesale, and thus on another day he breaks out concerning one of the delegates from South Carolina: "a perfect Bob-o-Lin-
coln, a swallow, a sparrow, a peacock; excessively

vain, excessively weak, and excessively variable and
unsteady, jejune, inane, and puerile." We need
not believe that the gentleman over whom John
Adams pours so many epithets was quite as bad as
all that, when we look in the face those extraordinary and peevish words he wrote many years later
about George Washington: "I will be bolder still,
Mr. Taylor. Would Washington have ever been
commander of the revolutionary army or president
of the United States, if he had not married the rich
widow of Mr. Custis?" He also laid Jefferson's
eminence to his wife's dollars. Was it because of
the rich widow of Mr. Custis that John Adams
had himself stood on the floor of Congress and
nominated Washington for commander-in-chief?
The true reasons shall presently be made clear. It
may be gathered from the foregoing fragments
from the journal of the Continental Congress and
Adams's diary, that, beyond their common enemy,
England, North and South had little in common;
Virginia is claiming a prominence that angers New
England, Massachusetts (in the voice of John
Adams) is calling South Carolina a peacock, and
here is the feeling of Washington, soon after reaching Cambridge, as to the Massachusetts troops: "I
dare say the men would fight very well (if properly officered) although they are an exceeding dirty
and nasty people." What do we hear in all these

voices but the preluding strains of that Civil War
waiting ahead of them, almost ninety years down
the road of time? But on happier days, the Fathers
could sit in harmony, and perhaps we may deem
this a preluding strain of the ultimate, sorely-tested
Union: "Sep. 18, 1774. *Resolved unanimously.*
That this assembly feels deeply the suffering of
their countrymen in the Massachusetts Bay. . . ."
As to which, John Adams, in his nobler mood:
"This was one of the happiest days of my life.
. . . I saw the tears gush into the eyes of the old,
grave, pacific Quakers of Pennsylvania."

There was now no escape from war; Washington
went to Mount Vernon to prepare for it and was
there until called back to Congress in Philadelphia.
Again in his own words we read his mind, and the
quick march of events:—

"(January, 1775.) I had like to have forgot to
express my entire approbation of the laudable pursuit you are engaged in, of training an independent company. . . . A great number of very good
companies . . . are now in excellent training; the
people being resolved, altho' they wish for nothing
more ardently than . . . reconciliation . . . not to
purchase it at the expense of their liberty. . . .

"General Gage acknowledges . . . his men made
a very precipitate retreat from Concord. . . . A
brother's sword has been sheathed in a brother's

heart . . . and the peaceful plains of America are either to be drenched with blood, or inhabited by slaves. . . .

"(June 16, 1775.) Mr. President: Though I am truly sensitive of the high honor done me in this appointment, yet I feel great distress from a consciousness that my abilities . . . may not be equal to the . . . trust. . . . As to pay, Sir . . . as no pecuniary consideration could have prompted me to accept this . . . I do not wish to make any profit from it. I will keep an exact account of my expenses . . . and that is all I desire." (It was all he desired when he became President, also.) 18 June, 1775. "My dearest, I am now set down to write you on a subject which fills me with inexpressible concern." . . . 19 June, 1775 (To his brother): "Dear Jack,—I have been called upon by the unanimous voice of the colonies to take the command of the continental army. . . ." 19 June, 1775. "Dear Sir, I am now Imbarked on a tempestuous ocean, from whence perhaps no friendly harbor is to be found."

In spite of John Hancock's aspirations, his Massachusetts colleague, John Adams, had nominated the Virginian, triumphing over his frequent provincial narrowness with a generous and patriotic breadth. Since Braddock's defeat, Washington had been the greatest military figure in the colonies, his presence in Philadelphia had commanded new respect from those gathered there, and no other American had the authority and the following to override all jealousies and unite all views. John Adams saw this, and certainly of him it may be said that the good he did lives after him, while it is rather the evil that is interred with his bones.— When Washington heard his name come from Adams's lips, he took himself hastily out of the room; indeed, tradition says that he ran!

Since that May day in Williamsburg, 1759, when he blushed and took his seat in the House of Burgesses, sixteen years had gone over his head. He was now forty-three, his figure not more filled out than formerly—it never became so—and he was as straight and strong as ever. But although his plantation, and riding out before sunrise, and hauling the seine, duck shooting, fox-hunting, the oyster man,—all these had kept his health vigorous and his muscles trained, his eyes had looked upon approaching storm, his mind had been hot over the mother country's attack on the core of her child's liberty ("every act of authority of one man over another for which there is not absolute necessity is tyrannical," as Beccaria had put it), and his heart was sore night and day at the thought of breaking with that mother country. As he was leaving Philadelphia for Boston, came the news of

Bunker Hill, whereat he asked instantly, had the
militia behaved itself? "The liberties of the country are safe!" he exclaimed, on learning of the
men's brave conduct. He was a true prophet, but
much lay between that word and the goal; we may
be sure that his serenity of countenance, of which
so many have spoken, was a very grave serenity on
the 2d of July, 1775. As the guns of Cambridge
thundered for the arriving commander-in-chief,
whatever the bows he made to the admiring ladies
who looked on, such bows were something of a mask
to his preoccupations, when he saw the ragged,
gaunt, ill-disciplined troops, and remembered that
there had been a total of four barrels of powder in
New York when he passed through that city on his
way to this army. He took command the next day.

## V

From Napoleon's sneer at this war, which Washington now headed till December, 1783, to Lafayette's gallant and true retort to it, our Revolution
has borne every grade of epithet, kind and unkind
—as, a war of outposts, a war of skirmishes, a war
of retreats, a war of observation. The last is as just
a summary of so miscellaneous and outspread a
story as could well be hit on; but what matters any
name for a fact so portentous in human history? As
a war, its real military aspect is slowly emerging

from the myth of uninterrupted patriotism and
glory, universally taught to school children; its
political hue is still thickly painted and varnished
over by our writers. How many Americans know,
for instance, that England was at first extremely
lenient to us? fought us (until 1778) with one hand
in a glove, and an olive branch in the other? had
any wish rather than to crush us; had no wish save
to argue us back into the fold, and enforce argument
with an occasional victory not followed up? that in
our counsels, the determination to be deaf to such
argument was not at all times unswerving? and that
had England once consented to keep the hands of
Parliament off us, it is more than possible we should
have agreed to remain "within the empire" on those
terms? How many know the English politics that
lay behind Howe's conduct after the battles of Long
Island, Brandywine, and Germantown—lay behind
his whole easy-going sojourn in this country? Such
acts as the burning of Falmouth (now Portland)
and of Norfolk had not the sanction either of his
policy or Lord North's; but they made, in Washington's phrase, "fiery arguments" to sustain our
cause. For any American historian to speak the
truth on these matters is a very recent phenomenon,
their common design having been to leave out any
facts which spoil the political picture of the Revolution they chose to paint for our edification: a

ferocious, blood-shot tyrant on the one side, and on the other a compact band of "Fathers," down-trodden and martyred, yet with impeccable linen and bland legs. A wrong conception even of the Declaration of Independence as Jefferson's original invention still prevails; Jefferson merely drafted the document, expressing ideas well established in the contemporary air. Let us suppose that some leader of our own time were to write: "Three dangers to-day threaten the United States, any one of which could be fatal: unscrupulous Capital, destroying man's liberty to compete; unscrupulous Labor, destroying man's liberty to work; and undesirable Immigration, in which four years of naturalization are not going to counteract four hundred years of heredity. Unless the people check all of these, American liberty will become extinct";— if some one were to write a new Declaration of Independence, containing such sentences, he could not claim originality for them; he would be merely stating ideas that are among us everywhere. This is what Jefferson did, writing his sentences loosely, because the ideas they expressed were so familiar as to render exact definitions needless. Mr. Sydney George Fisher throws all these new lights upon the Revolution, which may perhaps (in its physical aspect) be likened to the gradual wanderings of a half-starved, half-naked man from Massachusetts

through New York, New Jersey, and Pennsylvania,
down to the Virginia peninsula, where at length he
corners his well-fed enemy, and defeats him.

Lucky it is that the day of desperation and distrust did not set in during those first months of
Washington's command. From the early moments
of his ordering Indian hunting shirts for the army,
in order to abolish provincial distinctions, and de-
ciding to besiege Boston, the men knew that a great
leader was come to them; this they never forgot
through the starvation and nakedness and penniless-
ness, through the dismal swamp of years through
which they followed him. Sometimes misery was
too much for them, and they went to their homes in
despair, unnerved for reënlistment, but in him they
did not cease to believe. With the Boston siege his
star rose high; he showed his best powers, and successfully. He read the mind of the foe, he was
marvellous in keeping his counsels secret from foe
and friend alike, and his moral courage was a sort
of tonic in the air. Then his star—and ours—began
to sink, helped by the great disappointment, which
followed the great hope of Canada's conquest. He
had written the noble and sorely troubled Schuyler,
whose experiences were proving almost too bitter
for him, ''We must bear up . . . and make the best
of mankind as they are, since we can not have them
as we wish,'' and to such words Philip Schuyler's

generous heart responded. But there was no one to
prop Washington thus, as the sky darkened more
and more; he had to be his own prop. At Long
Island he was outflanked and beaten, the star sank
lower, and by the end of 1776 was near setting,
when in the deep blackness of Congressional mis-
trust and military collapse, he risked everything,
and the bright light of Trenton and Princeton shone
upon the scene. Through all this his own powers
showed brilliantly; the English moved out of New
Jersey, and our cause had a precious breath of res-
pite, while his masterly strategy got him from the
British that title of "the Old Fox." But the star
had not really risen yet. The next summer, 1777,
saw what malcontents always called "Fabian policy"; nothing good happened, and then on September 10, Brandywine happened—something bad—
another beating from Howe, much like Long Island,
not a well-managed affair, only to be followed by
more of the same kind, bringing up with Germantown, October 5. It would have now been black indeed, but in twelve days came that great turning-
point, Burgoyne's surrender up in the North. At
this total failure of a whole British army, the world
began to look at us with new eyes; but it is hardly
unnatural that voices at home said, "No thanks to
Washington." His Brandywine was contrasted
with Saratoga, for which the specious Gates got the

credit which belonged to Schuyler and others, and then followed the Conway Cabal. This attempt at him behind his back Washington met in a manner such that there was presently nothing left of it or its disgraced leaders; nor did the Valley Forge winter witness nothing but evil—rotten as Congress became at this time, rotten as was the commissariat, rotten as was everything touched by the political hand. Important people began to see one or two important facts: that we had swallowed one British Army, and that no British Army, occupy though it might our cities for winter-quarters and dancing, appeared to be able to swallow us. There sat Washington at Valley Forge, cold, hungry, and ragged, no doubt,—but he sat there, unconquered, and meanwhile our famous and priceless friend Steuben had arrived with all his military knowledge from Frederick the Great, and was drilling those hungry patriots at Valley Forge. The result showed at Monmouth Court House, where Clinton, the new general, got a bad fright and made a narrow escape, which would have been no escape at all, but for the treachery of Charles Lee. The hand which France now took, though with D'Estaing and his ships it helped us to no victory, helped us most importantly at once in bringing to Europe a knowledge of George Washington. The French officers took news of his greatness and his honorable dealings back

with them, and in this way, too, through him our
star began to burn brighter. But some dismal
swamp was left. We sat for a while at a deadlock
with Britain, each side watching the other, and
then occurred the treason of Arnold, a dark and
heavy catastrophe. Although help from Lafayette
and France (where he had gone to stir it up) was
really about to come again, it was scarce yet visible,
even though Rochambeau was here, and the new
year, 1781, began in great darkness. The soldiers
had not been paid a penny for twelve months, and
man cannot live on patriotism alone. There was
mutiny, not unnatural, but of frightful menace,
which was met by the politicians with their cus-
tomary impotence in the face of any great reality.
This bred more mutiny, killed quickly by the
soldierly Wayne, and in two months the sky
brightened, never to cloud so thickly again. Money
came from France, and patriotism could at length
be fed and clothed; last of all, the sea was made ours
by France. This overbore the disaster of Gates at
Camden in the preceding August, already somewhat
cancelled by his great successor Greene, and by
September, Cornwallis was at Yorktown. It was a
terrible moment of suspense when the chance seemed
that the Count de Grasse, with his ships that gave
us the sea during that crucial moment, would sail
away before Washington could get down from the

Hudson to Virginia; but he waited, and on the 17th
of October Cornwallis surrendered. It was two
years before Great Britain signed the treaty of
peace, but with Yorktown ends the war.

Let us now look at Washington himself briefly,
through these years which have been briefly narrated. Once again we take sentences from his letters
covering many months:

"I know the unhappy predicament I stand in; I
know that much is expected of me; I know, that
without men, without arms, without ammunition,
without anything fit for the accommodation of a
soldier, little is to be done. . . . My own situation
feels so irksome to me at times, that, if I did not
consult the public good, more than my own tranquillity, I should long ere this have put everything
to the cast of a Dye. . . . Your letter of the 18th
descriptive of the jealousies and uneasiness which
exist among the Members of Congress is really
alarming—if the House is divided, the fabrick must
fall. . . . I am sensible a retreating army is encir-
cled with difficulties; that declining an engagement
subjects to general reproach, and that the common
cause may be affected by the discouragement it may
throw over the minds of the army. Nor am I insensible of the contrary effects, if a brilliant stroke
could be made with any possibility of success,
especially after our loss upon Long Island. But

. . . I can not think it safe . . . to adopt a different
system. . . . [This next is in a very dark hour.]
In confidence I tell you that I was never in such an
unhappy divided state since I was born. To lose all
comfort and happiness on the one hand, whilst I am
now fully persuaded that under such a system of
management as has been adopted, I can not have
the least chance for reputation, nor those allow-
ances made which the nature of the case requires;
and to be told, on the other, that if I leave the
service all will be lost, is, at the same time that I am
bereft of every peaceful moment, distressing in a
degree. But I will be done with the subject, with the
precaution to you that it is not a fit one to be pub-
licly known or discussed.''

Such was the quality of this heart: to know its
own plight as clearly as that, but to go straight on,
sinking self, both present and future, in the cause.
His secrecy, and the inner state of his mind, come
before us once in a vividness so impressive that over
the well-known, oft-told Delaware crossing a new
light is thrown. Just before that night, when politics, when the low state of the army, when the
dearth of all good news for many months, had at
last brought Washington to ''put everything to the
cast of a Dye,'' a Philadelphia acquaintance waited
upon him.

''In December I visited General Washington in

company with Col. Jos. Reed at the General's quarters about 10 miles above Bristol, and four from the Delaware. I spent a night at a farm house near to him and the next morning passed near an hour with him in private. He appeared much depressed and lamented the ragged and dissolving state of his army in affecting terms. I gave him assurances of the disposition of Congress to support him, under his present difficulties and distresses. While I was talking to him I observed him to play with his pen and ink upon several small pieces of paper. One of them by accident fell upon the floor near my feet. I was struck with the inscription upon it. It was 'victory or death.'

"On the following evening I was ordered by General Cadwalader to attend the Militia at Dunk's ferry. An attempt was made to cross the Delaware at that place . . . in order to co-operate with General Washington . . . in an attack upon the Hessians. . . . Floating ice rendered the passage of the river impracticable. . . . The next morning we heard that General Washington had been more successful . . . and taken one thousand Hessians. . . . I found that the countersign of his troops of the surprize of Trenton was, 'Victory or Death.' "

For "near an hour," then, the Philadelphia acquaintance, Dr. Benjamin Rush, had sat with Washington, assuring him of support, and Wash-

ington, with his mind full of Trenton that was to
happen in thirty-six hours, had sat listening (or
perhaps not listening much) and scrawling on little
scraps of paper. Was "victory or death" upon all
of them, or was he writing various countersigns to
see how they looked? At all events, there in the
three words is his secret mind before Trenton, while
the visitor discoursed about Congress; that pen-
scribbling is a very striking instance of how, when
the spirit of a man is supremely concentrated, he
will often perform trivial, almost unconscious acts.
To one familiar with the relations between Washington and Dr. Rush, it may occur that these lay at
the bottom of Washington's silence; but this would
be an error. Dr. Rush's attack on Dr. Shippen was
still to come and to create in Washington the distrust made final by Dr. Rush's attack on himself in
the anonymous letter written to Patrick Henry. All
that—the face professions of friendship and the
back-hand stab, Henry's loyalty and Washington's
deeply moved response to it—was still more than a
year off, and Washington would have been silent to
any visitor about Trenton, for silence as to his plans
was inveterate with him.

His bright letter to Congress the day after Trenton is a marked change from his dark letter the day
before it, and in still greater contrast with the whole
darkness of his mind disclosed to his brother during

that black December, 1776: "If every nerve is not strained to recruit the new army . . . I think the game is pretty nearly up. . . . However, under a full persuasion of the justice of our cause, I can not entertain an Idea that it will finally sink, tho' it may remain for some time under a cloud."

Von Moltke, whose word may be considered as final authority, called Washington one of the world's very greatest strategists, adding: "No finer movement was ever executed than the retreat across the Jerseys, the return across the Delaware a first time, and then a second, so as to draw out the enemy in a long thin line." Genius usually seeks its element as a duck the water, as Alexander looked for "more worlds to conquer." Washington always looked for Mount Vernon, always went back to his crops and his trees, made war as a public duty only; and his military achievement seems to be the fruit, not so much of military genius, but of those great powers and qualities of firmness, sagacity, observation, and detail, which he showed in every undertaking either of war or peace, and of his invaluable training in the Indian wars.

That constitution, of whose strength he wrote Dinwiddie in the early days, was called upon to meet demands as heavy as those upon his mind;—after the defeat on Long Island, for instance, he was on horseback during the greater part of forty-eight

hours, and his ability to laugh uproariously sometimes must have been an excellent, if rare, relief for
him. General Putnam provided one great chance
for it during the Boston winter, while several
treacheries were being unearthed. Of one of these
they found the missing link at quite a serious crisis,
when the hiding of our lack of powder was near
being ruined by spies. The missing link turned out
to be a large fat woman, and so triumphant and
eager was large fat Putnam to bring her quickly to
headquarters, that he clapped her a-straddle in
front of him on his horse. Washington, looking out
of an upper window, saw this sight approaching,
—an important Puritan General apparently bearing the spoils of war brazenly before all eyes—and
it is said that he was entirely overcome, but had
mastered his gravity by the time the missing link
was deposited in his presence by her assiduous and
innocent captor. In the midst of matters so few of
which are laughing matters, it would be agreeable
to tell and dwell upon every instance of Washington's mirth; but the knowledge must be enough, that
he could and did laugh, and that the incident of the
fat woman is not the solitary jet of hilarity whose
radiance twinkles in that dusk. Of the dearth of
powder in one instance an idea may be had by this:
owing to a mistake in the report of the Massachusetts committee, instead of four hundred and eighty-

five quarter casks of powder, there were only thirty-
five half barrels, or not a half a pound to a man. It
is recorded that when Washington heard this, he
did not utter a word for half an hour. But presently
in the midst of more trials we find him quoting
poetry, philosophically: "I will not lament or repine . . . because I am in a great measure a convert
to Mr. Pope's opinion, that whatever is, is
right. . . ."

To quote poetry, or make any literary allusion, is
so rare a thing with him in his letters, that an instance of it is always a slight surprise. He writes to
young Custis at his schooling, "For, as Shakespeare
says, 'He that robs me of my good name enriches
not himself, but renders me poor indeed,' or words
to that effect." In another place he serves himself
of Hamlet with "in my mind's eye." He several
times uses "under the rose," and all these seem
natural, save for their great scarcity. But it is quite
astonishing to come upon *"in petto,"* and one comes
upon it only once. He seems fond of the word
"maugre," already archaic in his day, and one
wonders where he got it; but there is one phrase he
uses with such evident relish, and so repeatedly, that
to omit the instances here would be to lose not only
an interesting little fact of his style, but a sign of
something deep in the man. It is at one of the
deeply disheartening hours of the war that he writes

George Mason from Middlebrook, 27 March, 1779:
"I have seen without despondency even for a
moment . . . the hours which America have stiled
her gloomy ones, but I have beheld no day since the
commencement of hostilities that I have thought her
liberties in such eminent danger as at present. . . .
Why do they not come forth to save their Country?
let this voice my dear Sir call upon you—Jefferson
and others—do not from a mistaken opinion that we
are about to set down under our own vine, & our
own fig tree, let our hitherto noble struggle end in
ignom'y—believe me when I tell you there is danger
of it—I have pretty good reasons for thinking that
Administration a little while ago had resolved to
give the matter up, and negociate a peace with us
upon almost any terms; but I shall be much mistaken if they do not now from the present state of
our currency and dissensions & other circumstances
push matters to the utmost extremity. . . ." In
that ringing appeal, the pet phrase appears for the
first time, it would seem. And now, let the others
come :—

(To Oliver Wolcott.) ". . . but if ever this hap-
pens, it must be under my own vine and fig-tree."

(To David Humphreys.) ". . . but neither came
to hand until long after I had left the chair of
Government, and was seated in the shade of my own
Vine and Figtree."

(To Lafayette.) ". . . With what concerns myself personally, I shall not take up your time further
than to add, that I have once more retreated to the
shades of my own vine and fig Tree."

(To Mrs. Sarah Fairfax.) "Worn out in a manner by the toils of my past labor, I am again seated
under my vine and fig-tree."

(To John Adams.) "It is unnecessary, I hope,
for me in that event to express the satisfaction it
will give Mrs. Washington and me to see Mrs.
Adams and yourself, and company in the shade of
our vine and fig-tree."

(To J. Q. Adams.) "I am now as you supposed
the case would be when you then wrote, seated under
the shade of my Vine and Fig-tree."

We may smile, but what a pathos is in these
reiterations! They all belong to his last years at
Mount Vernon.

One other locution seems to have pleased him,
and of its several appearances we give but one, from
a letter to Charles Cotesworth Pinckney: "P.S.—
Mr. Lewis and Nelly Custis fulfilled their matri-
monial engagement on the 22nd of February. In
consequence the former, having relinquished the
Lapp of Mars for the sports of Venus, has declined
a Military appointment."

Scattered through his letters during the period of
the Revolution, we come upon various apologies for

real or seeming neglect in hospitality, or cordiality
—for failures, in short, to show people the attention
which they had the right to expect; in these apologies he mentions, among other things, the weight of
his correspondence. As much as he could he used
secretaries, giving them memorandums, sketched
quickly in his own handsome hand, with many
abbreviations: ''The time of my arrival—The situation of the Troops—Works—& things in general
—Enemy on Bunkers Hill. . . . Express gratitude
for the rediness wch. the Congress & diff. Commit-
tees have shown to make everything as convenient
and agreeable as possible. . . .'' But of course he
could not use secretaries for everything. His brilliant contemporaries and colleagues not seldom
shook their heads solemnly over his writings; but
they need not have done so. They did so because his
sagacity and moral weight so stood out during these
distracting times that such gifted men as Jefferson
and Hamilton fell dupe to a very human instinct—
they wanted to find something which they could do
better than he could, and they picked out his English style. They were quite mistaken. While these
collateral fathers of the country could *spell* words
better than Washington, *use* words better they could
not. No better prose than his was written, when he
took time to it. There are periods during the war
(and periods afterward) when controlled passion or

deep concern causes his language to reach the highest level of expression and dignity. During the Conway Cabal, in his papers public and private the style rises so that it would be hard to find writing to surpass it. Specimens are too long to quote, but they are easy to find in the sixth volume of his correspondence (edited by Ford), where the reader may look especially at a letter to Gates, page 362, and one to Bryan Fairfax, page 389. For the lesson to political manners of to-day that it contains, we quote this fragment from the same volume. "If General Conway means, by cool receptions, mentioned in the last paragraph of his letter of the 31st ultimo, that I did not receive him in the language of a warm and cordial friend, I readily confess the charge. I did not, nor shall I ever, till I am capable of the arts of dissimulation. These I despise, and my feelings will not permit me to make professions of friendship to the man I deem my enemy, and whose system of conduct forbids it." Conway was at last run to earth, and his tendered resignation was accepted when he did not mean it to be. This so disconcerted him that he wrote saying his language had been misconstrued: "I am an Irishman," he protests, "and learnt my English in France." This is probably our only heritage of pure gayety from the whole contemptible business, in which certain professed friends cut so poor a figure, and Lafayette, Richard Henry Lee, and Patrick Henry shine so brightly. We close this brief account of Washington's prose style with one final sentence to show both his own modesty on this head, and how needless such modesty was:—

"When I look back to the length of this letter, I am so much astonished and frightened at it myself that I have not the courage to give it a careful reading for the purpose of corrections. You must, therefore, receive it with all its imperfections, accompanied with this assurance, that, though there may be inaccuracies in the letter, there is not a single defect in the friendship."

His whole bitterness over the Conway Cabal is contained in one sentence written to Governor Livingston, but omitted from the second draft of the letter: "With many, it is a sufficient cause to . . . wish the ruin of a man, because he has been happy enough to be the object of *his country's favor.*" He underlined the words himself, and this, with the subsequent omission of the whole, shows in a stroke his feelings and his reticence. We have another graphic instance of character in two notes written General Howe on the same day, concerning the shorter of which the Chevalier de Pontgibaud gives the following account:—

"The British, occupied in the pleasures which they found in Philadelphia, allowed us to pass the winter in tranquillity; they never spoke of the camp at Valley Forges, except to joke about it, and we for our part might almost have forgotten that we were in the presence of an enemy if we had not received a chance visitor. We were at table at headquarters—that is to say in the mill, which was comfortable enough—one day, when a fine sporting dog, which was evidently lost, came to ask for some dinner. On its collar were the words, *General Howe*. It was the British Commander's dog. It was sent back under a flag of truce, and General Howe replied by a warm letter of thanks to this act of courtesy on the part of his enemy, our general.'' This was Washington's note to Howe: ''General Washington's compliments to General Howe,—does himself the pleasure to return him a dog, which accidentally fell into his hands, and, by the inscription on the collar, appears to belong to General Howe.'' The official one that was written on the same day, October 6, 1777, concerning depredations attributed to Americans and done by British, contains language severely different, and would give no hint of dogs and flags of truce: Washington the commander, writing to Howe the commander, was one thing; Washington the courteous lover of sport, writing to Howe the owner of a lost dog, was another.

The Chevalier de Pontgibaud errs, as the reader

will have perceived, as to the place where this happened, for they were not at Valley Forge so early as October, and it was "near Pennibecker's Mill"— the Chevalier is right about there being a mill, and the fact that at Valley Forge there was also a mill is what probably led to this immaterial confusion. Washington's note proves the accuracy of the story, and the following anecdotes also narrated by de Pontgibaud are as vivid, and may equally be accepted, whether they occurred at "Valley Forges," as he called it, or not exactly there.

"One day we were at dinner at headquarters; an Indian entered the room, walked round the table, and seized a large joint of hot roast beef. We were all much surprised, but General Washington gave orders that he was not to be interfered with, saying laughingly, that it was apparently the dinner hour of this Mutius Scævola of the New World. On another occasion a chief came into the room where our Generals were holding a council of war. Washington, who was tall and very strong, rose, coolly took the Indian by the shoulders, and put him outside the door."

It may be that the degrading dissensions, incompetences, and dishonesties of Congress reached, about the Valley Forge period, a low-water mark that they never surpassed in war time (in peace time later, they did); but however that is, it can

scarce too much be insisted that our Revolution was
not a sort of flawless architectural fabric, made
wholly of colonial pillars and patriotism, but that
it had a sordid, squalid back-door and premises, of
which Gouverneur Morris writes Washington:
"Had our Saviour addressed a Chapter to the
Rulers of Mankind . . . I am persuaded his good
sense would have dictated this text—be not wise
overmuch. . . . The most precious moments pass
unheeded away like vulgar Things." Such is a gentle way of putting it; but hearken now to the anything but gentle Washington:—

(To James Warren, 31 March, 1779.) "The measure of iniquity is not yet filled . . . Speculation,
Peculation . . . afford . . . glaring instances of its
being the interest . . . of too many . . . to continue the war. . . . Shall a few designing men . . .
to gratify their own avarice, overset the goodly
fabric we have been rearing at the expense of so
much time, blood, & treasure? And shall we at last
become the victims of our own abominable lust of
gain? Forbid it Heaven! Forbid it all & every
State in the Union! . . . Our cause is noble. It is
the cause of mankind. . . ."

If absolutely nothing from his letters were collected save passages devoted to the political iniq-
uities, such passages would make a volume; so
would the passages asking for powder, and so those

asking for food and clothing, and a fourth could be filled with his protests against short enlistments, by reason of which his army was constantly dissolving in his hands. A Harvard degree, and a medal from Congress (in one of its more amiable and coherent moods) could not have gone very far to compensate him for what he was enduring.

"General Fry, that wonderful man, has made a most wonderful hand of it. . . . He has drawn three hundred and seventy five dollars, never done one day's duty, scarce been three times out of his home. . . . I have made a pretty good slam among such kind of officers . . . having broke one Colo. and two Captains for cowardly behavior . . . two Captains for drawing more provisions and pay than they had men . . . and one for being absent from his post when the enemy appeared. . . . Different regiments were upon the point of cutting each other's throats for a few standing locusts near their encampment, to dress their victuals with . . . it will be very difficult to prevail on them to remain a moment longer than they choose themselves. . . . Such a dearth of public spirit . . . I never saw before . . . and pray God I may never be witness to again. . . . The Connecticut troops will be prevailed upon to stay no longer than their terms. . . . Could I have forseen what I have, and am likely to experience, no consideration upon earth should have induced me to accept this command . . . but we must bear up . . . and make the best of mankind as they are, since we can not have them as we wish.'' This last philosophical sentence, it will be remembered, he wrote his friend General Schuyler, and it is a thought we come upon several times. Thus, after blowing off his just rage, would he reënter the splendid poise of his staying-power. It is exhilarating to find him taking a ''good slam'' with his muscles also on a certain occasion. He rode into camp suddenly upon a fist fight, begun with mere snow-balling, between some newly arrived Virginians and some New England men. Such a fight was of vital menace to the army, full of northern and southern jealousies. He leaped from his horse, took two Virginians by their throats, and shook them in such fashion, talking the while, that in a very few moments he and they were the only people left in sight.

No excess of investigation (and there can be such a thing) would enable us to put our finger upon the moment of the lowest ebb of Washington's staying-power during this war of rags and starvation. There were several moments of very low ebb; but tradition hands one down from Valley Forge, connected with a white-handled pen-knife, upon which small instrument the fortunes of America would seem during that moment to have hung. Together with a clock, whose hands were stopped by an attending physician in Washington's bedroom as he expired, and which have marked that hour ever since, this white-handled pen-knife is treasured in the Masonic museum at Alexandria, and was given to Washington by his mother when he was about fifteen years old. It will be remembered that, but for her, he would have entered the navy in 1746. His brother Lawrence had obtained for him a midshipman's warrant, but it had gone much further than that; the boy's kit had been carried aboard, and he was himself on the point of following it, when a messenger from his mother overtook him, and brought him her final word, so imploring, or so peremptory—tradition says not which—that he abandoned his project, and went home—back to more school and mathematics, as has been related early in these pages. In the next order for supplies that his mother sent to England, she asked for a "good pen-knife." This, when it came, she gave to the boy in token of his recent signal submission to her, adding, "Always obey your superiors." He carried the token all his life, and to some of his intimates he from time to time explained its significance. One day at Valley Forge, when the more than half-naked men had eaten no meat for many days, and when Congress had failed once more to provide, or even to suggest any way for getting, food

and clothes, the ebb was reached, and Washington
wrote his resignation as commander-in-chief of the
army. Among the generals sitting in council, Henry
Knox spoke out, reminding him of the pen-knife,
and upon Washington's asking what that had to do
with it, he said: ''You were always to obey your
superiors. You were commanded to lead this army.
No one has commanded you to cease leading it.''
Washington paused, and then answered, ''There is
something in that. I will think it over.'' Half an
hour later, he tore his resignation to pieces.

The rumour of what he said and what he did
through all these hours of struggle and desperation, spread wide and far from the centre of them,
spread across the seas, spread to all distant corners
of travel, and the blunt remark of a Scotchman in
Key West bears witness to what was thought of
him by enemies of his cause. News had come that
Washington was captured, and the Scot was sorry
to hear of this, ''for he is too gude a mon to be
hangit,'' he said, feeling sure this would be the
prisoner's fate. His renown rose to a new height in
that passage of diplomacy that he had with Lord
Howe over the manner in which he should be styled
in letters by the British commander; after he had
sent back a communication addressed ''To George
Washington Esq^{re},'' and a second, where the point
was still dodged, ''To George Washington Esq^{re}.

&c. &c. &c.,'' Congress thanked him for thus assert-
ing his dignity, and further resolved that they
"have such entire confidence in his judgment . . .
they will give him no particular directions." American dignity is not invariably so well guarded by its
soldiers, or understood by its civilians. As for the
"entire confidence" of Congress, that short-winded
affair soon gave out—it spent its time in giving out
and reviving;—presently this "entire confidence"
was near shifting to Gates, and soon after Gates
had blown over came what may have been the
heaviest blow, personally, that Washington sus-
tained—Arnold's treason. About this, when he
learned it, Washington remarked, simply and quietly: "Whom can we trust now?" Arnold had been
a gallant fighter, in fact, a brilliant fighter, and
Washington and others (John Adams, for instance)
were of opinion that his services had met poor recognition; thus, when the bottom falseness of his
nature was revealed suddenly, it was for a moment
overwhelming. From such experiences he got the
habit of feeding upon all good news that came, and
making the most possible of this, and the least possible of ill news; but if good news had been his only
nourishment, he would often have starved, and the
truth is, he fed upon his own inexhaustible determination, becoming at times in the general dearth of
money, food, clothing, and powder, himself the only

sinews of war that we possessed. Yet, with this for-
titude, he wept like a child when he saw, across the
Hudson, his soldiers being bayoneted. In some
actions he so recklessly forgot himself, that they
seized his bridle and led him away from needless
exposure. It seems, too, that he was imprudent
(certainly once) in cold blood. Shortly before
Brandywine, he was reconnoitring the country near
Wilmington, with Greene and Lafayette. They had
ridden all day, and night came, and with night a
storm, from the fury of which they sought shelter
in a farm-house. The enemy was everywhere, likely
to capture them at any moment, and this Washington knew; but nothing that Greene or Lafayette
said could induce him to budge. He stayed on, im-
movably, and to their dismay stayed all night. As
they rode away in the morning, he candidly agreed
that this had been most unwise and dangerous! We
can only guess at what made him do such a thing.
Probably he was dog-tired, and found the rain very
wet, and the fire very dry and pleasant, and told
himself that nobody would be looking for him in
such a storm, or that if they did, he would kill them.
Or perhaps he told himself nothing at all beyond
that he would not budge from the fire and the house
till morning, let Greene and Lafayette protest as
they would. Upon an occasion very similar to this,
and at about the same period of the war, we have his

own word for his fatigue when he stopped at night-
fall again at a house in this same tract of country.
It is handed down by the descendants of this house,
that one of its daughters, then a little girl, was all
curiosity and excitement upon learning who it was
that her elders were harboring. She begged hard for
a sight of the great visitor, and she had her wish.
"Well, my dear," said the general, "you see a very
tired man in a *very* dirty shirt."

Since a tale of Washington incautious has been
told, let it be set off by one showing the shrewd wiles
of that strategy for which he earned his name of
"the Old Fox," from those whom he so constantly
outwitted. During the Morristown winter, when the
army was all but gone to nothing—some three thousand men were the whole of it—it was discovered a
spy from Howe in New York was in the camp.
Washington gave orders that he should be warmly
treated, as if taken into friendship and confidence;
he also ordered all his colonels to make false returns
of their regiments' strength. These papers, reporting *twelve* thousand men on duty, were left in very
accessible pigeon-holes in the adjutant's office. One
day, while the spy was chatting with the adjutant,
a message came from the commander requesting to
see the adjutant at once. Thus carefully left alone
in the room, the spy punctually performed the trick
he was intended to perform, got at the reports, read

them through (comfortable time for this was allowed him), and went off happy to Howe in New
York with the official figures of Washington's
strength—twelve thousand. Soon after this another
spy came, a young officer, who discovered the truth,
and returned tq Howe with it. But he was not
believed; had not his predecessor secured the official
figures? Not only was he discredited, but severely
treated for being so incompetent and dangerous a
spy.

So Washington was not caught at Morristown, or
at the farm-house, or anywhere, and amid rags and
starvation brought the war through; hindered by a
host of difficulties, helped by many things—brave
generals, patriotic civilians, devoted soldiers, and
not a little by the Whig party in England; but most
of all by the huge shoulders of his own endurance.

How did his face look at the end of it that noon
in New York at a tavern down by the Whitehall
Ferry, the 4th of December, 1783? He was there to
say good-by to his assembled generals, privately,
among themselves, before starting for Congress to
resign his commission. A boat waited to take him
over the river on his way to Annapolis. In that tavern, Fraunce's Tavern, his generals had gathered,
—Knox, and the rest of those dear to him. The
sight of these brothers-at-arms, as he entered the
room, deprived him of utterance; again he stood in

that overcome silence that the House of Burgesses
had known in him long ago, but it was not any more
the young, blushing, brown-haired Washington.
His back was not bent with the load carried since
July 3, 1775, and never set down; but he had looked
upon much death, much need, much distress, and he
had known disloyalty, ingratitude, and treason
once, in the likeness of a trusted fellow-soldier, during that long journey. Benedict Arnold cannot
have failed to drive something into Washington's
soul that was not there before, and now, in the tavern room with those who had gone through so much
with him, what sort of face did he turn upon these
comrades? It must have been a face of many memories. He filled a glass of wine and drank them his
farewell. "I cannot come to each of you to take my
leave," he said, "but shall be obliged if each of
you will come and take me by the hand." No word
was spoken after that. Each took him by the hand,
and then all went down to the shore with him.
There they stood watching, until the boat took him
from their sight.

## VI

He seems to have counted himself now a man
whose hard work was done, whose rest was come,
a private man, for whom his vine and fig-tree were
at last in store: he seems not in the least to have

suspected that the new country had further need of
him, and he turned his face with relief to Mount
Vernon. The war had used his body hard; indeed,
his accidental allusion, in a very dangerous moment for him and the country, to his impaired
eyesight had saved the critical situation. Between
Yorktown and the signing of the peace, the much-
enduring army thought it was time for at least
a little pay, but Congress, no longer quite so frightened as in the days when it had fled from the
enemy's approach, preached sermons of resignation,
and suggested that the men placed too high a value
upon mere leaving their homes and giving their
lives. It was an incautious hour to choose for so
pious a lecture; to the men's angry minds it
occurred that there were not many steps to march
between themselves and the control of the Government, and they talked of their beloved leader as
Dictator. Washington's words quickly burst such
a bubble—but this did not stop the mutinous spirit,
and Congress, terrified once again by an army,
once again had none save Washington to look to
for the safety of its skin. It was a last chance for
the intriguing Gates to rise from the discredit of
his defeat at Camden, and he played it to the limit.
His underhand counsels to the men that their cause
was just (which it most assuredly was) and that
they must demand their rights, led them to open

sedition, and there was Washington where Gates wished him to be, of necessity protecting the Government which was in the wrong, and opposing the men who loved him, and who knew the Government was wrong. There was an hour set for him to meet them, and silence, instead of shouts, was their greeting to him. He had a written address prepared, but on rising to begin it, the text was dim to his eyes, and as he felt for his glasses in that moment during which his own influence and perhaps the country's fate trembled, he spoke simply to the gathered and sullen soldiers the first words that came to him: "I have not only grown gray but blind in your service." By this unpremeditated touch of nature the whole trouble was melted away, the formal address was needless, tears came to the men's cheeks, and they were willing to be patient for their leader's sake.

To Mount Vernon, then, he turned with his gray hairs and weakened sight, reaching there on Christmas eve, "to spend the remainder of my days," he wrote, "in cultivating the affections of good men, and in the practice of the domestic virtues. . . . A glass of wine and a bit of mutton are always ready . . . those who expect more will be disappointed." He presently revisited the trails of his youth, the backwoods, returning thence to the pastoral home existence that he supposed he was now free to enjoy. His daily rising was before the light, his correspondence done by the half-past seven breakfast, after which he rode over his fields until the half-past two dinner; this was followed by writing or by whist until dark. A guest speaks of his agreeableness, his delighting in anecdotes and adventures, silent upon all personal exploits; but Miss Custis saw another side, and described him as being constantly thoughtful and silent, with *lips moving*. Nothing said about him by any one at any time so conveys his inward isolation—inevitable consequence of a great man's moral and mental load—as this report of the moving lips. The money Congress now offered as reward for his services he declined, although his fortune was shrunk and his estate in dilapidation from the war. He speaks picturesquely of returning to find his buildings suffering from many wounds, and here is one of several allusions to straitened circumstances :—

". . . the bonds which were due to me before the Revolution, were discharged during the progress of it—with a few exceptions in depreciated paper (in some instances as low as a shilling in the pound). . . . Such has been the management of my Estate . . . as scarcely to support itself. . . . To keep myself out of debt I have found it expedient now and then to sell Lands. . . ." But, without dwelling further upon his business sense,

it is enough to add that he so redeemed his fortune
from its serious injuries as to die the second richest
man in America. His consummate insight regarding the western future of the country led him to
buy lands along all the great rivers, from the
Mohawk to the Kanawha, that he foresaw must
be the highways of travel and commerce; in some
cases such lands cost him five pounds the hundred
acres and were sold for five pounds the acre. Yet
his many directions as to buying and selling show
him to have been far above "sharp practice":
"Major Harrison must be sensible that no one can
be better acquainted with the land than I am; it
would be unnecessary therefore (if he has any
inclination to sell it) to ask a price which it will
not bear; but if he is disposed to take a reasonable
price, and will act the part of a frank and candid
man in fixing it, I would not have you higgle
(which I dislike) in making a bargain." Such were
his methods, and his fortune came by no means
like so many of those built upon dishonour at the
present day, but as the fair result of superior
sagacity and application. "Land rich," however,
as he died, he often lived "land poor," and with
income obliterated for a season in consequence of
patriotic neglect to watch his own affairs while
attending to the affairs of the nation; yet his need
of ready money did not check his aid to others in

need—the wife of Lafayette, for example, to whom he sent two hundred guineas at once on learning of her husband's imprisonment, or the sufferers from pestilence in Philadelphia to whom he offered assistance through Bishop White, "without ostentation or mention of my name," as he requests the bishop. Nor was it his fashion, as the mode is now, to put on the mask of a benefactor and thus disguised to label colleges and libraries with his own name, thus really leaving his money to himself. His gifts to education were gifts, and not advertisements or obituaries.

Intercolonial jealousies were, as we have seen, in full blossom already by 1776, and now they ripened quickly to full fruit. The common enemy gone, everybody had full time to fall upon his neighbour, and he did so, until they were all nearer to destroying their new country than King George had been; a republic is its own worst enemy, and we showed this then as we show it to-day. Washington would have despised the view expressed by a lesser public servant: "I had rather let the old ship sink, than keep pumping at her all the while;" therefore he tasted but little of his vine and fig-tree, and soon returned to the ship and the pumping. Lafayette, on December 30, 1777, had written to him: "Take away for an instant that modest diffidence of yourself . . . you would see very

plainly that if you were lost to America, there is
nobody who could keep the army and the revolution
for six months. There are open dissensions in
congress, parties who hate one another as much
as the common enemy.'' If Washington's modesty
forbade his believing this, the quarrelling factions
knew it to be true; cat and dog came running to
him, and soon he was presiding over the Constitutional Convention.

And now is the time to speak of the third car-
dinal influence in his life. It rests not on a level
with the others, coming upon Washington in the
full high-noon of his growth; but in clearing and
shaping his mind about what foundations our new
government should rest on, and how these should
be laid, its importance is unique. The other two
were influences upon *character*, the rules of civility
and the friendship of Fairfax; the third and last
is Alexander Hamilton. Of him, during the war,
we have this first glimpse recorded :—

''I noticed a youth, a mere stripling, small, slender, almost delicate in frame, marching beside a
piece of artillery with a cocked hat pulled down
over his eyes, apparently lost in thought, with his
hand resting on the cannon, and every now and
then patting it as he mused, as if it were a fa-
vourite horse or a pet plaything.'' This was Hamilton, not quite twenty years old. Washington, too,
caught sight of him at about this time, noticing

(amidst some disastrous hours of fighting) how
skilfully some earthworks were going forward under the direction of a young captain of artillery.
He sent for the young man, whose discourse so
struck him, that presently (March 1, 1777) he made
him aide-de-camp with the rank of lieutenant colonel, and next the young man, now twenty, was
conducting much of the correspondence of the
older man, now fifty-five. Nick-named "the little
lion" by a colleague, Hamilton was soon "my boy"
to Washington. The boy was already famous
through some pamphlets, and what war did for
the discipline and development of his genius—for
genius he had such as none other—must have been
priceless to him, and so to us. What his genius
did for Washington was equally inestimable. The
coming together of these two, the seasoned,
sagacious intelligence, and the winged, fiery intellect, may be likened to some beneficent chemical
union between acid and alkali, producing as it did
the very salt of constructive common sense. If
this had not, on the whole, prevailed during the
stormy years that were now to set in, we should
have been to-day but another nest of hornet republics, like the hemisphere to the south of us, or
else swallowed up by a foreign power. Among the
sundry passages that Washington wrote about the
case of the new country, we take two :—

(1785.) "The war . . . has terminated most

advantageously for America, and a fair field is presented to our view; but I confess to you freely, my dear Sir, that I do not think we possess wisdom or justice enough to cultivate it properly. Illiberality, jealousy, and local policy mix too much in all our public councils for the good government of the Union. . . . The confederation appears . . . little more than a shadow . . . and Congress a nugatory body. . . . To me . . . it is one of the most extraordinary things in nature, that we should confederate as a nation, and yet be afraid to give the rulers of that nation who are the creatures of our making, appointed for a limited and short duration, and who are amenable for every action . . . sufficient powers to order and direct the affairs of the same. . . . By such policy . . . we are descending into the vale of confusion and darkness. That we have it in our power to become one of the most respectable nations upon earth, admits, in my humble opinion, of no doubt, if we would but pursue a wise, just, and liberal policy towards one another, and keep good faith with the rest of the world.'' (This sentence about ''good faith'' arose from his seeing the populist instinct not to pay your creditors rapidly growing.) Later, 1787: ''I almost despair of seeing a favourable issue to the proceedings of our convention, and do therefore repent having had any agency in the business.

The men who oppose a strong and energetic government, are in my opinion narrow-minded politicians. . . . The apprehension expressed by them, that the *people* will not accede to the form proposed, is the *ostensible*, not the *real* cause of opposition. . . . I am sorry you went away. I wish you were back." (This is to Hamilton.)

We find more angry and more despondent words than these in his letters at this time, but what has been quoted clearly shows his thoughts and feelings; presently the Constitution was adopted, and next, on April 14, 1789, a deputation from Congress waited on him at Mount Vernon, and formally announced that he was unanimously elected first President of the United States. "I wish," he replied, "that there may not be reason for regretting the choice." To Knox, his war comrade, he wrote: "In confidence, I tell *you* . . . that my movement to the chair of Government will be accompanied by feelings not unlike those of a culprit who is going to the place of his execution."

Vine and fig-tree were left behind in this spirit, in which there is nowhere to be found any sign of elation, but only personal regret and unwillingness, and a solemn dedication of self to the new needs of the country. The greeting he met, the universal shout of loyalty, when he stepped forth upon the balcony at his inauguration, caused him

to falter and sit down, and this brought a silence
as intense and universal as the cheering had been.
Thus he took his oath, and then turned to enter a
maze of troubles of every size and shape, from the
petty follies about the etiquette of his receptions to
the question how the American people could be
persuaded to pay their debts both domestic and
foreign. There was scarce a meanness too small or
a blindness too great for some of the chief citizens
of that day; and everything was brought to him,
or if it was not brought, the responsibility of dealing with it fell upon him nevertheless, and he got
the blame whenever any one was not pleased. "We
have probably had too good an opinion of human
nature in forming our confederation," he had written a little while before, and what he now began
to experience was not likely to disabuse him of
this opinion, but only to send him back to the same
philosophy he had once preached to General Schuyler to "make the best of mankind as they are, since
we can not have them as we wish." Etiquette,
then (as to which Hamilton, Adams, and Jefferson
all differed), had to be established, just how much
and how little there should be, and this practical
question was complicated not only by differences
of opinion, but by not a little false and ridiculous
gossip. Some of this is eagerly set down by Jefferson in his book of malice that he called *Anas,* where-

in he has written himself down a character to which
his worst enemy could scarce add a syllable. He
describes Washington and Mrs. Washington as
sitting on a sort of throne during a ball, at which,
as a matter of fact, they were on the floor dancing
during the whole evening. Indian troubles, secretly
fomented by the English, harassed our frontier,
and a great disaster was suffered, the news of which
caused one of those outbreaks of violent emotion
to which Washington was subject. His general
health showed signs of the worries he lived daily
in, among which the greatest, possibly, was the
problem of finance. The doctrine of not paying
your debts was offered in various sugar-coated
forms of rhetoric as a *principle* that should form
part of our national policy. Taxation was felt to
be an insult to American freedom, and a strong
party came into existence whose aim may be fairly
said to have been to resolve our Republic into a
''society for the avoidance of personal obligations''
—to quote the admirable words of Mr. Oliver in
his study of Alexander Hamilton. ''According to
the practice of demagogy,'' this writer continues,
''the doctrine of repudiation was . . . raised to a
higher moral plane. In the twilight of words and
phrases the seductive idea, like a lady of doubtful
virtue and waning beauty, was arranged in a char-
itable and becoming shadow. . . .'' Thomas Jeffer-

son favored all these things; he worked out one of
his ingenious quackeries to show the iniquity of
creating a national debt. We had no moral right
to make a loan that our children must pay; he
produced arithmetic to show that nineteen years is
the length of a generation, and he advocated that
any debt still unpaid after nineteen years should
be extinguished. It may be imagined how attractive such a scheme would be to a "society for the
avoidance of personal obligations," and how dear
to the hearts of "the people" Jefferson thus made
himself; it may also be imagined with what hearti-
ness Holland, or any other country, would have
responded to our application for money, if such
doctrines had prevailed. Shea's Rebellion—one of
our paper-money episodes of insanity, and at core
a local phase of repudiation—had a few years
earlier revealed the ideas of the society for the
avoidance of personal obligation, and for this
demonstration Jefferson had nothing but praise.
"God forbid," he said, "that we should be twenty
years without a rebellion. . . . The tree of liberty
must be refreshed from time to time with the blood
of patriots and tyrants. It is its natural manure."
From this sprightly and vivacious doctrine he ex-
cepted himself; when Tarleton and his raiders came
too near the Virginia legislature, he fled with a
promptness that showed conclusively he had no

intention his own blood should refresh the tree of liberty. The still more comprehensive doctrine, that if any man happened to dislike any law, it was his American perquisite and sacred right to break such law, was another of the menacing undercurrents during Washington's first term, and during his second it broke out in the Whiskey Insurrection. It was deemed by true Jeffersonians, such as Edmund Randolph, a despotic outrage upon liberty that troops should be sent to enforce order and obedience to the law. These are the "principles" that we have inherited from Thomas Jefferson—if it can be said that he had any fixed principles—and it is no wonder that he remains a popular idol; the real wonder is, that Washington, who threw his whole force against such principles, and with Hamilton's help largely defeated them, should remain a popular idol too. It is most natural that Hamilton, the greatest benefactor our young country knew, except Washington, should have no popularity whatever, although his greatness is beginning at last to emerge and establish itself in the general knowledge of mankind. Lest the reader, not fresh from any first-hand examination of Jefferson, but only aware of him through a sort of traditional hearsay, should be tempted to doubt the phrase above as to Jefferson's instability of convictions, let him read and ponder the following sentence :—

"When any one state in the American union re-fuses obedience to the Confederation to which they have bound themselves the rest have the natural right to compell it to obedience." The expounder of states-rights wrote this. It may be found in Ford's "Writings of Thomas Jefferson," Vol. iv, page 147.

Through Thomas Jefferson there ran one sincere thread of belief—his faith in mankind, and for this he is beloved of the multitude without any investigation as to how much concrete benefit to mankind resulted from his faith. Phrases indeed he coined—nobody more elegantly or prolifically, but (again to use Mr. Oliver's words) "no power could translate them into policy or law, because they did not correspond with any translatable human facts. For the greater part they were only words, and for the rest they were the fancies of a poet." We, far away from the malice and disloyalty Jefferson measured out not alone to his political foes, but to friends of whose reputation he grew jealous, can feel his personal fascination. Such keen outlook, such vivacious curiosity as to all things, such engaging fancy and diction, make him a wonderful being; he stands the incomparable dabbler, the illustrious dilettante, of his day. As the writer of the Declaration of Independence, he lives permanently with those great founders of our Republic, whom we shall

never forget; as the consummator of the Louisiana
Purchase (a total departure from his own "principles") we owe him equal or deeper gratitude;
but if his political coherence, his constructive statesmanship, is examined, it crumbles away, leaving
nothing but a faith in mankind amid a cloud of
dust.

Worry over the mischief made, and the more
mischief attempted, by those who corresponded in
that day to the "green-backers," the "farmers'
alliance," and the "populists" of later days, impaired Washington's health, and also fatigued and
disenchanted him in his ceaseless effort to set the
infant Republic on its legs. The infant Republic
struggled tooth and nail against this; in fact,
toward every measure adopted for its soundness
and permanence, the infant Republic may be
likened in its conduct to an ill-conditioned, squall-
ing brat, disgusting all save its most patient guard-
ians. Washington would have been very glad to
be free of the whole business; but the brat, genu-
inely scared lest the parent whom it had been biting
and scratching should abandon it to its own devices,
clung to him, not in gratitude, but in terror. Even
Jefferson, who had been opposed to the Administration's policy, and, though a member of the cabinet,
was encouraging newspaper attacks upon it—if
he did not actually dictate many of the articles him-

self—even Jefferson wished Washington to stay.
Jefferson's most useful trait, perhaps, was a power
to drop all his theories in the face of a crisis, and
do the practical thing. "North and South will hang
together if they have you to hang on," he said;
and Washington stayed—but here is how he felt:—

"To say I feel pleasure from the prospect of
commencing another tour of duty would be a departure from truth; for, however it might savor
of affectation in the opinion of the world (who, by
the by, can only guess at my sentiments, as it never
has been troubled with them), my particular and
confidential friends well know, that it was after a
long and painful conflict in my own breast, that I
was withheld (by considerations which are not
necessary to be mentioned) from requesting in time,
that no vote might be thrown away upon me, it
being my fixed determination to return to the walks
of private life at the end of my term."

But he could not do so, and well it is for our
present existence that he did not do so. Nothing
but the confidence and love he filled the people with
over the heads and beyond the voices of the papers
and politicians could have tided us through the
dangers which now not only came to us without invitation, but which the papers and politicians also
loudly invited. Washington was not a party man;
he says of himself, "party disputes are now carried

to such a length, and truth is so enveloped in mist
and false representation, that it is extremely difficult to know through what channel to seek it. This
difficulty to one who is of no party, and whose sole
wish is to pursue with undeviating steps a path,
which would lead this country to respectability,
wealth, and happiness, is exceedingly to be
lamented.'' In this same spirit he made appointments, writing a favorite nephew who had asked
him for one, ''however deserving you may be . . .
your standing would not justify my nomination
of you . . . in preference to some of the ablest and
most esteemed . . . lawyers. . . . My political conduct in nominations, even if I were uninfluenced by
principle, must be exceedingly circumspect. . . .''
The use of his name in a Maryland election brought
to the culprit one of his very severe rebukes: ''I
was not a little displeased to find . . . my name
had been freely used by you or your friends . . .
when I had never associated your name and the
election together. . . . There had been the most
scrupulous and pointed caution . . . on my part
not to express a sentiment respecting the fitness or
unfitness of any candidate for representation. . . .
The exercise of an influence would be highly improper; as the people ought to be entirely at liberty
to chuse whom they pleased to represent them in
Congress.'' But this highmindedness was lost upon

the screaming infant Republic, feverish with that disease not yet exterminated, and always fatal if not kept in check, the disease of plebiscitis. Sickened by the treatment he received, Washington speaks without reserve, once, to Jefferson: ". . . nor did I believe until lately . . . that, while I was using my utmost exertions to establish a national character of our own, independent, as far as our obligations and justice would permit, of every nation of the earth, . . . every act of my administration would be tortured . . . and that too in such exaggerated and indecent terms as could scarcely be applied to a Nero, a notorious defaulter, or even to a common pickpocket."

A delirious dread of Washington's becoming king—he pronounced it insane himself to Jefferson, who feared, or made believe to fear it—was continually fomented by the papers, of which he took no public notice; but his letters are full of the evidences of his feeling. "In a word," he writes Edmund Randolph before the scandal of the French minister had ended their relations, "if the government and the offices of it are to be the constant theme for newspaper abuse, and this too without condescending to investigate the motives or the facts, it will be impossible, I conceive, for any man living to manage the helm or to keep the machine together."

It is curious to read those newspapers of the
1790's and see how much time has moderated the
violence of words, though not at all the poison of
slander and sensation. It could not be printed to-
day that "the eldest son of Satan, Albert Gallatin,
arrived in town yesterday afternoon." They dared
not go so far with Washington's name, but they
spent much ingenuity upon him. In a sort of bur-
lesque dictionary, published in Freneau's *Gazette*,
Philadelphia, 24 April, 1793, we find: *"Great man.
Excellent judge of horse-flesh."* And again, "Va-
lerius" (or "Brutus" or "Publius") writes: "If
the *form* of monarchy was exalted among us, a national love of liberty would rally all around the
standard of opposition, except the minions of the
idol." Once more: "The temple of Liberty, like
that of Vesta, should never be without a centinel.
. . . Were I to see public servants excluding private
citizens from their tables, I should not hesitate to
sound the alarm." We may wonder, if every American had the right to dine with his President, how
long the cook would stay. Let us see what the hap-
less public servant had to say about this last accu-
sation: "Between the hours of three and four every
Tuesday, I am prepared to receive. . . . Gentlemen,
often in great numbers, come and go, chat with each
other, and act as they please. . . . Similar . . . are
the visits every Friday afternoon to Mrs. Washing-

ton, where I always am.—These—and a dinner once
a week to as many as my table will hold—are as
much, if not more, than I am able to undergo; for
I have already had, within less than a year, two
severe attacks—the last one worse than the first. A
third, more than probably, will put me to sleep with
my fathers." To this, let the following, with its unconscious pathos and irony be appended. "31st
July, 1797. Dear Sir: I am alone at *present* . . .
unless some one pops in unexpectedly, Mrs. Washington and myself will do what I believe has not
been done in the last twenty years by us—that is to
set down to dinner by ourselves."

During these first momentous years, two forces—
the perennial forces of our Commonwealth, the Federal power and the State power—were to be appor-
tioned and proportioned, and between these Washington's strength was continually ground. Any
event, any question, whether domestic or foreign,
set them raging. Had the centrifugal force out-
balanced the other, we should have been all tire and
no axle; the wheels of the Republic would have sunk
in splinters. Those who dreaded on the other hand
that we should be all axle and no tire, pushed their
dread rather fantastically; but certainly, if the
wheels are to stay sound and turning, we need the
perpetual, adjusted equilibrium of those two forces;
the United States are a federation, each one remain-

ing a whole as regards each of the others, though it be a part as regards the whole. But upon Washington the grinding told, and with the ill consequences to his health came some not surprising signs of increasing irascibility. Several references to violent outbreaks on his part have been made; the news of St. Clair's defeat by the Indians had caused one of these, narrated by the single person in whose presence it occurred. Of another, which took place in the presence of the whole cabinet, Jefferson gives the account. "Knox in a foolish, Incoherent sort of speech introduced the Pasquinade lately printed, called the funeral of George Washington, and James Wilson, King and Judge, &c., where the President was placed on a guillotine. The President was much inflamed, got into one of those passions when he can not command himself, ran on to the personal abuse which had been bestowed upon him, defied any man on earth to produce one single act of his since he had been in the government which was not done on the purest motives, that he had never repented but once the having slipped the moment of resigning his office, and that was every moment since, that *by God* he would rather be in his grave than in his present situation. That he had rather be on his farm than to be made *emperor of the world* and yet that they were charging him with wanting to be a King. . . . He ended in this high tone.

There was a pause. Some difficulty in resuming our question.''

Poor, beset, bull-baited Washington! The mind, even all these years after, feels a shock of anger and shame that he should have tasted an ingratitude so insensate and bestial. The "voice of the people," Jefferson's divine guide, has never (in this country) more clearly shown that it can be, on occasion, the voice of hell.

A cartoon, showing Washington upon the guillotine (which was never an instrument of execution in this country), is curiously significant of how closely the French Revolution grazed us, how mixed and kneaded in it was with our popular imagination. No other foreign event has ever come so near us, has ever so occupied the general mind, has ever so endangered our own existence. That convulsion, while it was ripping France open and tearing it down, and while it was threatening to shake the whole house of Europe to pieces, sent undulations over here that would infallibly have split our walls too, but for the firm back of Washington, propped against them. He distrusted the French Revolution from the first, when Jefferson was gleefully hailing it as the dawn of the millennium. His letters, wishing the cause of liberty well, betray a reserve as to the method in which the French are seeking liberty, and this doubt increases until it ends in horrified repudiation of what was being done; "the summit of despotism" is his brief opinion of it. But there was a loud party here that did not discriminate; it was mainly composed of those who regarded taxation as a symptom of monarchy, and understood a republic to mean the right to break any law that displeased you; but we must do these people what justice we can. There was a wide and righteous gratitude to France for what she had done to help our own Revolution, and there was a treaty with her, besides an equally wide and natural hatred of England, with whom France was presently at war. Where these people failed to discriminate was in their inability to see that the France who had helped us, the France of Lafayette and Rochambeau, of Louis XVI, was not the France they wished to befriend in return; *our* France had been pulled down by a mob, and it was not even to its ruins, but to the mob, that American sympathy was directed. Bache's paper of May 25, 1793, expresses the general belief in saying: "The fact will be found to be, that the French understand the principles of a free government—that the English do not." Nothing that Washington did brought him bitterer hate than his stand for neutrality when England went to war with France. The French party here would have rushed this tottering young country into a European strife. Some one from Pittsburgh writes

to Freneau's *Gazette*: "Louis Capet has lost his
Caput. From my use of a pun, it may seem that I
think lightly of his fate. I certainly do." And the
same paper later addresses Washington, "Sir . . .
The cause of France is the cause of man, and neutrality is desertion. . . . I doubt much whether it
is the disposition of the United States to preserve
the conduct you enjoin. . . . The American mind
is indignant, and needs but to be roused a little to
go to war with England and assist France." For a
while the volatile Jefferson busily connived at all
this, busily befriended the French envoy, the im-
pudent and meddlesome Genêt. We cannot go into
the case of the *Little Sarah*, that was fitted out to
aid France and sailed away under Jefferson's nose.
There can be little doubt he was uncandid with
Washington about this; a sentence in a letter from
Washington to Henry Lee is highly significant; but
when he came face to face with the results of his
ill-judged patronage of Genêt, and found that this
political adventurer proposed to appeal to the
American people against the decision of the President, he came back to his senses for a while. Genêt,
according to his successor, Fauchet, showed "more
personal hatred for Washington than love for
France." Fauchet himself turned out a rascal later,
and Adet, who followed him, was as bad. These
people, sent to us by French "liberty," form a

curious contrast with Lafayette, de Grasse, Rochambeau, Chastellux, and the others who came to
us from French "despotism." Washington's proc-
lamation of neutrality saved us from a peril that
might well have been fatal, and the "American
mind," in spite of the newspaper, accepted the President's judgment. "I'll tell you what," said John
Adams to the Spanish minister, Yrujo, a young man
very free and easy in his manners, as Washington
describes him, "the French republic will not last
three months"; and Adams shook his finger at
Yrujo. Jefferson quotes this with malicious relish,
as showing what a fool Adams was. The French republic did last longer than three months. It was
proclaimed in 1792. In one year they abolished the
Calendar and the Christian era, renamed all the
months, and started a new era with the year one.
They then abolished Christianity itself; Robespierre
dancing in front of the image of Reason, while
flowers were strewed about. This performance was
entitled the "Picnic of the Supreme Being." Then
they cut off Robespierre's head—he was not advanced enough for them—and children were given
toy guillotines, which cut off dolls' heads, from
which spurted red syrup. This was the real France,
with which the "American mind" felt such sympathy; a France of rivers of blood, in which danced
monkeys and assassins. Even the flighty Jefferson's

vision of the millennium was troubled during the
Reign of Terror, and we find him writing a very
mixed metaphor to the effect that "the arm of the
people" is "blind to a certain degree." After 1792,
France was republic, directorate, consulate, monarchy, and empire, changing its form of government
ten times in eighty years. We recall and assemble
these familiar facts in order that against their back-
ground the reader may more instantly see the value
of Washington's neutrality, and the folly of the
very powerful and clamorous party who denounced
it; but to see these things fully, the newspapers of
that day should be read. From the many echoes of
doubt and distrust in our stability caused by the
resistance to taxation and the sympathy with the
French Revolution, we select a few lines written
from Congress by the same Jeremiah Smith who
became chief justice of New Hampshire:—

"You perceive that we have been, I may say still
are, on the edge of a precipice, ready to take a leap
into the abyss of confusion. . . . God knows how
this ship of ours will sail, when the present pilot
quits the helm. If we may judge from present appearances, she will inevitably founder."

From the pilot's own letters we select and place
together for the last time some sentences dealing
with a few of his problems—many of them still our

problems—and showing the man himself after his
encounter with them.

"The difference of conduct between the friends
and foes of . . . good government, is . . . that the
latter are always working like bees to distil their
poison; whilst the former, depending often times
*too much* and *too long* upon the sense and good disposition of the people to work conviction, neglect
the means of effecting it. . . . My opinion with respect to emigration is that except of useful mechanics and some particular description of men or
professions, there is no need of encouragement,
while the policy or advantage of its taking place in a
body . . . may be much questioned: for by so doing, they retain the Language, habits and principles
(good or bad) which they bring with them. . . .
Never forget that we are Americans, the remem-
brance of which will convince us that we ought not
to be French or English. . . . [The following shows
how early a certain habit of visitors from abroad
began.] The remarks of a foreign Count are such
as do no credit to his judgment, and as little to his
heart. They are the superficial observations of a
few months' residence, and an insult to the inhabitants of a country, where he has received much
more attention and civility than he seems to merit.
. . ." [It was also bound to begin early, that rep-

resentatives elected to represent should misrepresent those who elected them, and this seems to have come to a considerable head at the time of Jay's treaty with England, an understanding which France did her best to prevent.] The treaty, said Washington, "does not rise to all our wishes, yet it appears to be calculated to procure to the United States such advantages as entitle it to our acceptance. . . . People living at a distance know not how to believe it possible that . . . representatives . . . can speak a language which is repugnant to the sense of their constituents. . . . Whatever my own opinion may be . . . it . . . will continue to be my earnest desire to learn, and, as far as consistent, to comply with, the public sentiment; but it is on *great* occasions *only*, and after time has been given for cool and deliberate reflection, that the *real* voice of the people can be known. . . . I am sure the mass of citizens in these United States *mean well*, and I firmly believe they will always *act well* whenever they can obtain a right understanding . . . but in some parts of the Union, where the sentiments of their delegates and leaders are adverse to the government and great pains are taken to inculcate a belief that their rights are assailed and their liberties endangered, it is not easy to accomplish this; especially, as is the case invariably, when the inventors and abettors of pernicious measures use infinite more industry in disseminating the poison, than the well-disposed part of the community to furnish the antidote. . . ."

As has been said, he began as a man of no party, but became inevitably ranged with the Federalists; his political affinity with Hamilton, his affection for him—ever warmer as the years went on—and his modest recognition of Hamilton's superior gifts in statesmanship, led him to go to his friend with every question that he was pondering, even small ones. Adet, the third unsatisfactory envoy from France, had published a letter to the Secretary of State:—

". . . whether the *publication* in the manner it appears is by order of the Directory, or an act of his own, is yet to be learnt. If the first, he has executed a duty only; if the latter, he exceeded it, and is himself responsible for the indignity offered to this Government by such publication, without allowing it time to reply. . . . In either case, should there be in your opinion any difference in my reception and treatment of that Minister in his visits at the public Rooms (I have not seen him yet, nor do not expect to do it before Tuesday next)—and what difference should be made if any?"

To which Hamilton answers:—

"The true rule on this point would be to receive

the Minister at your levees with a *dignified reserve,*
holding an *exact medium* between an *offensive cold-
ness* and *cordiality.* The point is a nice one to be
hit, but no one will know how to do it better than
the President.''

We dwell not upon his Farewell Address, his
own idea and work—though it benefited by the
criticism of Hamilton; it needs no mention here;
we finish with a few further examples of his opinions. ''I was in hopes that motives of policy as
well as other good reasons supported by the direful
effects of slavery . . . would have operated to produce a total prohibition of the importation of slaves.
. . . Were it not that I am principled against selling negroes . . . I would not in twelve months
from this date be possessed of one, as a slave. I
shall be happily mistaken if they are not found to
be very troublesome species of property ere many
years pass over our heads. . . . We are *all* the children of the same country. . . . Our interest . . . is
the same. . . . My system . . . has uniformly been
. . . to contemplate the United States as one great
whole . . . for sure I am, if this country is preserved in tranquillity twenty years longer, it may
bid defiance in a just cause to any power whatever;
such in that time will be its population, wealth and
resources. . . . [The next regards the Federal City
which he had in mind.] I take the liberty of send-

ing you the plan of a new city, situated about the centre of the Union of these States, which is designated for the permanent seat of government. . . . A century hence if this country keeps united (and it is surely its policy and interest to do it) will produce a city, though not so large as London, yet of a magnitude inferior to few others in Europe, on the banks of the Potomac . . . where elegant buildings are erecting and in forwardness for the reception of Congress in the year 1800. . . . [This concerns his third term.] It would be a matter of sore regret to me, if I could believe that a serious thought was turned towards me . . . for, although I have abundant cause to be thankful for the good health with which I am blessed, yet I am not insensible to my declination in other respects. It would be criminal, therefore, in me, although it would be the wish of my countrymen . . . to accept an office . . . which another would discharge with more ability.''

This is the person whom they pictured on the guillotine; the author of that Farewell Address more times printed than any American state document; and this is the person of whom the newspaper, Bache's *Aurora,* said upon his retiring from the presidency: ''If ever a Nation was debauched by a man, the American Nation has been debauched by Washington.''

So much patience of mind seems never to have
belonged to any other great public man; to take
difficult thoughts, one by one, and march slowly
to their end, and so to reach conclusions which were
impregnable then, and which time itself has left
unassailed, this was his preëminent quality. Very
different he was from the ingenious, better-educated
Jefferson, whose mind leaped lightly to attractive
generalizations, which the ruthless test of actuality
finds to be mostly rubbish. The two may be styled
the hare and the tortoise of our Independence. One
other great quality comes forth from all Washington's deeds and words, like a beautiful glow; its
lustre seems to shine in every page that he writes,
and in all his dealings with men, with ideas, with
himself; it is the quality of simplicity. Our fathers
had it more than we of to-day, and it would be well
for us if we could regain it. The Englishman of
to-day is superior to us in it; he has in general,
no matter what his station, a quiet way of doing
and of being, of letting himself alone, that we in
general lack. We cannot seem to let ourselves
alone; we must talk when there is nothing to say;
we must joke—especially we must joke—when there
is no need for it, and when nobody asks to be
entertained. This is the nervousness of democracy;
we are uncertain if the other man thinks we are
"as good" as he is; therefore we must prove that

we are, at first sight, by some sort of performance. Such doubt never occurs to the established man, to the man whose case is proven; he is not thinking about what we think of him. So the Indian, so the frontiersman, so the true gentleman, does not live in this restlessness. Nor did Washington; and therefore he moved always in simplicity, that balanced and wholesome ease of the spirit, which when it comes among those who must be showing off from moment to moment, shines like a quiet star upon fireworks.

And how did the man who had been twice Presi- dent now look? The descriptions of him belonging to this period tell of changes. Less mention is made of his agreeable smile, his cheerful serenity, his pleasant talk; it is his gravity, his reticence, even his melancholy—this is the record. Is it surprising in one who, when reticence was during an angry moment broken, had declared that he would rather be in his grave than in his present situation? If Arnold had added a furrow to his face, there must have been many new ones by this time; but here is one word about himself, written in considerable indignation, that unveils something of the depths he usually concealed: "Whether you have, upon any occasion, expressed yourself in disrespectful terms of me, I know not—it has never been the subject of my enquiry. If nothing impeaching my

honor or honesty is said, I care little for the rest.
I have pursued one uniform course for threescore
years, and am happy in *believing* that the world
have thought it a right one—of it's being so, I am so
well satisfied myself, that I shall not depart from
it by turning either to the right or to the left, until
I arrive at the end of my pilgrimage.''

An agreeable and graphic account of Washington
the President is given in the privately published
memoirs of Mr. Charles Biddle, a distinguished
Philadelphian of that day:—

''When he was elected President of the United
States, he lived during the whole of the time that
he was in Philadelphia nearly opposite to me. At
that time I saw him almost daily. I frequently
attended levees to introduce some friend or acquaintance, and called sometimes with Governor
Mifflin. The General always behaved politely to the
Governor, but it appeared to me he had not forgotten the Governor's opposition to him during the
Revolutionary war. He was a most elegant figure of
a man, with so much dignity of manners, that no
person whatever could take any improper liberties
with him. I have heard Mr. Robert Morris, who
was as intimate with him as any man in America,
say that he was the only man in whose presence
he felt any awe. You would seldom see a frown
or a smile on his countenance, his air was serious

and reflecting, yet I have seen him in the theatre laugh heartily. Dr. Forrest, who laughs a great deal, desired me one night at the theatre, to look at General Washington. 'See how he laughs, by the Lord he must be a gentleman.' The General was in the next box, and I believe heard him. He was much more cheerful when he was retiring from office of President than I had ever seen him before. Commodore Barry, Major Jackson, and myself were appointed a Committee of the Society of Cincinnati to wait upon him with a copy of an address, and to know when it would be convenient for the Society to wait upon him. He received us with great good humor, and laughing, told us that he had heard Governor Morris (I believe of New Jersey) say that when he knew gentlemen were going to call on him with an address, he sent to beg they would bring an answer. If this were done to him, he observed that it would save him a great deal of trouble. He was in Philadelphia a short time before he died, and I thought he never looked better than he did at that time. . . . He was called the American Fabius, but Fabius was not equal to George Washington. He suffered Tarentum to be pillaged when it was traitorously delivered to him, and his opposition and jealousy of Scipio rendered the Roman unequal to the American hero.''

It is upon the day of his release, the day when

public burdens fell from him, and the vine and
fig-tree began to draw near in his hopes, that we
shall take our farewell look at him. His successor,
John Adams, had finished taking his oath; Washington turned to leave the assembly, and at this
sight, all who could do so crowded from their places
to the hall, that they might see the last of him. He
passed through their cheering to the street, where
in answer he waved his hat, "his countenance
radiant with benignity, his gray hairs streaming in
the wind." It is from the lips of an eye-witness that
Irving gives this account. "The crowd followed
him to his door; there, turning round, his countenance assumed a grave and almost melancholy expression, his eyes were bathed in tears, his emotions
were too great for utterance, and only by gestures
could he indicate his thanks and convey his farewell
blessing."

Three years of quiet he lived to see, and then was
dead after brief illness, able to ride his horse to
within three days of the end, and ready to take
the command against France in case of war. He
seemed to know his illness was indeed the end,
although, during the twenty hours of its progress,
he let them try what remedies they wished; when
at last his friend Dr. Craik sat on his bed, and
took his head in his lap, he said with difficulty:
"Doctor, I am dying, and have been dying for a
long time, but I am not afraid to die."

## VII

Go, when the day is fine, down the river to Mount
Vernon. There, following the path up from the
shore among the trees, you will slowly come to
where his tomb is, the simple vault half up the
hill, which vines partly cover, built according to
his directions. From this you will still ascend
among grass and trees, and pass up by old buildings, old barns, an old coach-house with the coach
in it, and so come to the level green upon which
the house gives with its connecting side offices at
either flank. Inside the house, all through the rooms
of bygone comfort so comfortable still, so mellowed
with the long sense of home, you will feel the
memory of his presence strangely, and how much
his house is like him. He seems to come from his
battles and his austere fame, and to be here by the
fireplace. Here are some of his very books on the
shelves, here the stairs he went up and down, here
in the hall his swords, and the key of the Bastille
that Lafayette sent to him. Upstairs is the room
he died in, and the bed; still above this chamber,
the little room where Martha Washington lived her
last years after his death, with its window looking
out upon the tomb where he was first laid. Everything, every object, every corner and step, seems
to bring him close, not in the way of speaking of
him or breathing of him, as some memorial places

seem to speak and breathe their significance; a
silence fills these passages and rooms, a particular
motionlessness, that is not changed or disturbed by
the constant moving back and forth of the visitors.
What they do, their voices, their stopping and bend-
ing to look at this or that, does not seem to affect,
or even to reach, the strange influence that sur-
rounds them. It is an exquisite and friendly serenity
which bathes one's sense, that brings him so near,
that seems to be charged all through with some
meaning or message of beneficence and reassurance,
but nothing that could be put into words.

And then, not staying too long in the house, stroll
out upon the grounds. Look away to the woods
and fields, whence he rode home from hunting with
Lord Fairfax, over which his maturer gaze roved
as he watched his crops and his fences, and to
which his majestic figure came back with pleasure
and relief from the burdens and the admiration of
the world. Turn into his garden and look at the
walls and the walks he planned, the box hedges, the
trees, the flower-beds, the great order and the great
sweetness everywhere. And among all this, still
the visitors are moving, looking, speaking, the men,
women, and children from every corner of the country, some plain and rustic enough, some laughing
and talking louder than need be, but all drawn here
to see it, to remember it, to take it home with them,

to be in their own ways and according to their several lights touched by it, and no more disturbing the lovely peace of it than they disturbed the house. For again, as in the house, only if possible more marvellously still, there comes from the trees, the box hedges, the glimpses of the river, that serenity with its message of beneficence and reassurance, that cannot be put into words. It seems to lay a hand upon all and make them, for a moment, one. You may spend an hour, you may spend a day, wandering, sitting, feeling this gentle power of the place; you may come back another time, it meets you, you cannot dispel it by familiarity.

Then go down the hill again, past the old buildings, past the tomb, among the trees to the shore. As you recede from the shore, you watch the place grow into the compactness of distance, and then it seems to speak: "I am still here, my countrymen, to do you what good I can." And as you think of this, and bless the devotion of those whose piety and care treasure the place, and keep it sacred and beautiful, you turn and look up the expanding river. From behind a wooded point, silent and far, the Nation's roof-tree, the dome of the Capitol, moves into sight. A turn of the river, and it moves behind the point again; but now, on the other side of the wide water distance, rises that shaft built to his memory, almost seeming to grow from the stream itself; presently, shaft and dome stand out against the sky, with the Federal City that he prophesied, Union's hearth-stone and high-seat, stretching between them.

*"He that has light within his own clear breast*
*May sit i' the centre, and enjoy bright day."*

# CHRONOLOGY

| DATE | EVENTS | AGE |
|------|--------|-----|
| 1657 | Emigration of John and Lawrence Washington to Virginia . . . . . . . . | |
| 1694 | Augustine Washington, father of George Washington, born . . . . . . . . . | |
| 1732 | Feb. 22. George Washington born in Westmoreland County, Virginia . . . | |
| 1733-4 | Family moved to the farm now known as Mount Vernon . . . . . . . . . . . | 1-2 |
| 1743 | April 12. Death of Augustine Washington | 11 |
| 1743 | George sent to live with his half-brother Augustine at birthplace . . . . . . . | 11 |
| 1743-5 | Mansion built and named Mount Vernon by his half-brother Lawrence . . . . | 13 |
| 1745 | He returned to live with his mother at Fredericksburg. School . . . . . . . | 13 |
| 1746 | At his mother's request gave up entering the navy . . . . . . . . . . . . | 14 |
| 1748 | March 11. Became surveyor for Lord Fairfax . . . . . . . . . . . . . | 16 |
| 1749 | Appointed public surveyor . . . . . . . | 17 |
| 1751 | Military inspector with rank of Major to protect Virginia frontier against French and Indians . . . . . . . . . . . | 19 |
| 1751 | Sept. Journey with invalid brother Lawrence to Barbadoes . . . . . . . . . | 19 |
| 1752 | Adjutant-general. Sept. 26, Mount Vernon left him by Lawrence . . . . . . | 20 |
| 1753 | Mission to frontier. Venango, Duquesne | 21 |
| 1754 | Lieutenant-colonel. Great Meadows campaign. Venango, Duquesne. Ill health. Sojourns at Mount Vernon . . . . . . | 22 |

| DATE | EVENTS | AGE |
|---|---|---|
| 1755 | Aide-de-camp to General Braddock. Venango, Duquesne. Commander-in-chief of the Virginia forces . . . . . . . | 23 |
| 1756 | Military mission to New York and Boston | 24 |
| 1758 | Ill health. Courtship. March to the Ohio. Resigned commission . . . . . | 26 |
| 1759 | Jan. 6. Married to Martha Dandridge Custis . . . . . . . . . . . . . . | 26 |
| 1759 | May. Took seat in House of Burgesses . | 27 |
| 1765 | Commissioner for settling the military accounts of the colony . . . . . . . . | 33 |
| 1770 | Journey to the Ohio and Kenawha rivers | 38 |
| 1774 | Member of the Virginia Convention on the points at issue between England and the Colonies . . . . . . . . . . | 42 |
| 1774 | Sept. Member of the First Continental Congress . . . . . . . . . . . . | 42 |
| 1775 | May 10. Member of the Second Continental Congress. June 15. Commander-in-chief. July 3. Took command at Cambridge. Siege of Boston . | 43 |
| 1776 | Mar. 17. Boston evacuated by British. Aug. 27. Battle of Long Island. Dec. 26. Battle of Trenton. Dec. 27. Invested by Congress with dictatorial powers . . . . . . . . . . . . | 44 |
| 1777 | Jan. 3. Battle of Princeton. Winter quarters at Morristown. Sept 11. Battle of Brandywine. Oct. 4. Battle of Germantown . . . . . . . . . . | 44–45 |
| 1778 | Winter quarters at Valley Forge. Conway Cabal. June 28. Battle of Monmouth Court-house . . . . . . . . . . . | |
| | Arrival of d'Estaing. Winter quarters at Middlebrook . . . . . . . . . . | 45–46 |

| DATE | EVENTS | AGE |
|------|--------|-----|
| 1779 | July 16. Capture of Stony Point . . . . | 47 |
| 1780 | Arnold's treason . . . . . . . . . . . | 48 |
| 1781 | Jan. 1. Pennsylvania troops mutiny. Oct. 19. Surrender of Cornwallis at Yorktown . . . . . . . . . . . . | 49 |
| 1782 | Threatening sedition of army and talk of dictator . . . . . . . . . . . . . | 50 |
| 1783 | April 19. Peace proclaimed to the army. Nov. 2. His farewell to the army. Dec. 4. His farewell to his generals. Dec. 23. He resigned his commission at Annapolis. Dec. 24. Home to Mount Vernon . . . . . . . . . . . . . | 51 |
| 1784 | Journey to the western country. . . . . | 52 |
| 1787 | May 14. Delegate to Constitutional Convention at Philadelphia. President of the Convention . . . . . . . . | 55 |
| 1789 | President of the United States. Apr. 30. Inaugurated in New York. Journey through Eastern States . . . . . . | 57 |
| 1791 | Journey through Southern States . . . . | 59 |
| 1793 | Second time President of United States. The episode of Genêt, minister from France . . . . . . . . . . . . | 61 |
| 1796 | Sept. 17. Farewell address to the people of the United States . . . . . . . | 64 |
| 1797 | Home to Mount Vernon. Troubles with France. Preparations for war . . . . | 65 |
| 1798 | July 3. Commander-in-chief of the armies of the United States . . . . . . . | 66 |
| 1799 | Dec. 14. Died at Mount Vernon . . . . | 67 |

# BIBLIOGRAPHY

THE WRITINGS OF GEORGE WASHINGTON. Collected and edited
by Worthington Chauncey Ford. Letter-press Edition.
G. P. Putnam's Sons. New York. 1893.

THE LIFE OF WASHINGTON, by Washington Irving. In 8
volumes. G. P. Putnam's Sons. New York. 1855–59.

THE TRUE HISTORY OF THE REVOLUTION, by Sydney George
Fisher. J. B. Lippincott Co. Philadelphia. 1902.

ALEXANDER HAMILTON, by Frederick Scott Oliver. G. P.
Putnam's Sons. New York. 1907.

PATRICK HENRY, by Moses Coit Tyler. Houghton, Mifflin
& Company. Boston. 1887.

THE TRUE THOMAS JEFFERSON, by William Eleroy Curtis.
J. B. Lippincott Co. Philadelphia. 1901.

GEORGE WASHINGTON'S RULES OF CIVILITY, by Moncure D.
Conway. John W. Lovell Company. New York. 1890.

LIFE OF THE HON. JEREMIAH SMITH, LL.D., by John H.
Morison. Charles C. Little & James Brown. Boston.
1845.

And the memoirs, privately published, of Benjamin Rush
and Charles Biddle, together with the files of *Freneau's
Gazette* and *Bache's Aurora*, during the terms of Washington's presidency.